REVIEWS OF . . .

THE KASHA KNISH CAPER

"Like every good Jewish mother I hoped my son would be a lawyer or a doctor. After Jason finally became a lawyer I was so happy. Now, he wants to be an author too. Oy! What am I going to tell the other mothers when they ask what my son the lawyer is doing now? Winning some big case in court? No. He is selling his book. Such shame."

—**Jason's mother**

◇ ◇ ◇

"What? My grandson wrote a book? Why did I not know this until someone wanted a review from me? I am not reading his book until he fixes the VCR. I can't record my soaps. And, he got the title for his book from me since kasha is his favorite dish which I make for him. I better get credit in the book or else."

—**Jason's grandmother**

◇ ◇ ◇

"What is kasha? I don't get it. And why did he write an entire book about kasha?"

—**Bill** (Jason's non-Jewish friend)

"Jason won the sixth grade spelling bee. I was so proud of him. I hope he used spell check for his book, otherwise, I may tell him to return the certificate we gave him for winning the spelling bee."

—**Mrs. Harris** (Jason's Sixth Grade Teacher)

"Uncle Jay, if I read your book, will you buy me a new iPod?"

—**Jason's niece**

"It is definitely a book."

—**Anonymous Book Critic**

The Kasha Knish Caper

The Kasha Knish Caper

JASON GORDON

C7 Books, Inc.
Visit our website at www.C7Books.com

Printed in the United States of America.

Cover design by Larissa Hise Henoch
Inside design and formatting by Dawn Von Strolley Grove

Acknowledgments

I would first like to thank Carrie and Ari for the encouragement to write this book and to get it finished when I was fed up with moving commas around with each draft I reviewed. I also thank both of them for reviewing the first draft, which was in terrible shape compared to the book you will now read.

I would also like to thank Mr. Dreeson, my Eleventh grade English teacher, for inspiring me to want to write creatively.

And finally, the best writing partner a guy could have—my dog Sophie. Although she is only 20 lbs., she was nice enough to let me have half the chair while I sat in my office at home writing this book.

Chapter 1

Murray Goldstein came running into my office breathing heavy like he had just run a marathon.

"Rabbi, I need your help."

"Murray. Do you have an appointment?" asked Lola, my assistant.

"No, Lola. When trouble happens you don't make an appointment. You just go for help, so here I am. I need help."

"You do need help Murray, however, the Rabbi is not a psychiatrist and can't prescribe any medication for your problems. A few years on a couch is what you need."

"Lola, it is no great surprise that you are not married. No man would want to put up with your nagging until death do you part because he would know that your nagging would surely lead to an untimely death only if he were so lucky."

I could sit and watch Murray and Lola take shots at each other all day, but then I would not get any work done, and Lola would eventually knock Murray unconscious. She has a vicious right hook.

My name is Moshe Klein. I am a Rabbi and a private investigator. I played football in college and was headed for an NFL career when I blew out my knee in my senior year. I was not sure what to do after college, so I decided to become a cop. I spent ten years working as a cop in Miami, five of those years as a homicide detective. My father, his father and my three brothers are all rabbis. After ten years of being a cop I decided to go into the family business so I went to rabbinical school. Wearing a yarmulke as a cop was difficult at times because when I would run after criminals my yarmulke would often fall off. I was not a big fan of bobby pins—the secret to keeping a yarmulke on one's head while chasing assorted criminals. Miami's criminal element was not considerate enough to stop running away from me to give me an opportunity to pick up my yarmulke when it fell off so that I could continue the chase. I have learned that there is less running in my work as a Rabbi and a private investigator, thus my yarmulke is not as at risk for being run over in the middle of the road by an oncoming bus.

I got started as a private investigator because as members of my congregation learned that I was a former police officer, they would come to me for help with certain issues. After a while I figured I could be of greater assistance if I got my PI license.

Lola has worked with me for almost five years. She is of Italian decent and is a very tough lady. She is a single parent with a twelve year old daughter. Lola keeps my office running, keeps my clients from giving me too much trouble and loves to give Murray grief.

"O.k. Murray," I say in my calm, soothing Rabbi voice. "Take a seat and tell me what is wrong."

"Rabbi. Oy! Where to begin. I am not sleeping. I can't eat. I can't tell Deborah about this since it will worry her to no end. Rabbi, you know the woman. A typical Jewish mother. Does she need more things to worry about?"

"No Murray. She has plenty to worry about. She is married to you."

"Good point. Rabbi, you know that my deli is one

of the most popular delis in Miami Beach. I have been blessed. People come from all over to eat at my deli. Our early bird special is unparalleled. The number of Cadillacs and Lincoln Town Cars leaving Sunny Isles Beach and the condominiums on Collins Avenue every day at 4:30 PM to come to my deli strike fear in anyone under the age of sixty-five. I say a prayer each day to Seymour, the Angel of Safe Driving."

"Murray, I have never heard of Seymour, the Angel of Safe Driving. I think they would have taught me about such an Angel in rabbinical school."

"Rabbi, trust me. If one-hundred or more elderly Jews all drove to your synagogue every day around 5 PM, you would know about Seymour too."

"O.k. Murray. Continue with your story."

"One of the secrets of the success of my deli is the knishes. We have the best knishes anywhere in South Florida. I challenge anyone to find a better knish from here to West Palm Beach. Trust me, you can't. I have looked. I have the best."

"He does Rabbi. My Cindy can't even spell the word knish, but she has already decided that she is converting to Judaism when she grows up because Murray's knishes are so good," said Lola.

"Lola, it is nice that you and I can agree on something," said Murray.

"We both agree that I don't like you Murray. We agree on two things."

"Lola, sheket bevaka sha, hey!"

"Sorry, Rabbi."

Lola has picked up some Hebrew during her five years of working with me.

◇ ◇ ◇

"Murray, I don't understand what trouble you are in. Being a successful deli owner with excellent knishes is not a crime."

"True Rabbi, it is not. But the prices I charge for my knishes is a crime. They should cost twice as much. They are so good. Anyway, last week I was cleaning up after a particularly busy Thursday evening when three guys came into the deli. They were wearing very expensive Italian suits."

"I like them already," said Lola.

"They introduced themselves as Tony the Tilapia, Sammy the Salmon and Guido the Grouper. Tony the Tilapia said that some people they represent are in the knish business on a large scale. Tony said that they want in on my business, want a percentage of my profits and want me to sell them large quantities of knishes at cost," said Murray.

"Did they tell you why they want to purchase knishes from you?" I asked.

"They did not."

"What did you tell them?" Lola asked.

"I told them I was not interested. Tony then told me that I was going to give them what they want either the easy way or the hard way."

"Murray, is your life insurance paid up? You may want to increase the policy limits," said Lola.

"Rabbi, I'm scared. I don't know what these guys are going to do but I know it is not good. I don't want to give guys whose last names are all types of fish any part of my business, or sell them knishes at cost. Will you help me?" asked Murray.

"Let me see what I can find out."

Chapter 2

Later that day I was at the temple working on the torah class I was teaching that night. I could not focus on the class since I was worried about Murray. Why would guys named after types of fish wearing expensive Italian suits be interested in Murray's deli and his knishes?

I taught class that night to twenty students. We had a lively discussion about the torah portion of the week. After class I went home. As I walked in the door I was greeted by my wife Rachel and my two children, Jacob and Rebecca.

"Good evening Moshe. Nice to have you home," said Rachel.

"Hi Dad!!" said my kids in unison.

"Hi everyone. Did you have a good day?" I asked.

"Yes," all three said.

"Good. Let's sit down and have dinner and you can tell me about your day."

We sat down for dinner which consisted of chicken noodle soup, brisket and potatoes. Rachel's soup was legendary. It was not the reason I married Rachel, but it was a wonderful benefit of being married to her. Rebecca told me about the goings on of USY—her Jewish youth group. Jacob had a good practice for his basketball game on Thursday.

After dinner the kids went up to their rooms to finish their homework. Rachel and I sat down on the couch to talk.

"Moshe, you look troubled. Did something happen today?"

"Murray came to see me at the office."

"Did he bring knishes? His knishes are to die for."

"That is sort of the problem."

"What do you mean?" asked Rachel.

"Three guys in expensive Italian suits came to visit him last night when he was closing the deli."

"Lola must have liked them just for the expensive Italian suit part," said Rachel.

"Do you have a microphone in my office I am not aware of?" I asked.

"No silly. I just know Lola. Go on."

"Tony the Tilapia, the leader of the group, told Murray

that they want in on his business. They want a percentage of the profits and they want to buy knishes at cost."

"The percentage of profits I get, but why do they want to buy knishes? That seems odd," said Rachel.

"It does. That is the part I cannot figure out. Why would what I am guessing is some facet of the Italian mob want to buy large quantities of knishes?"

"Maybe Tony and his gang figure that since Murray's knishes are so popular they can sell them and make a profit by getting knishes at cost."

"But where would they sell the knishes? Knishes are not a hot item on the menu of an Italian restaurant. I will have the fettuccine alfredo and a kasha knish. I don't think those words have ever been uttered in an Italian restaurant." I decided I would pay money to watch someone give that order as it would be a proud moment for Murray and Jews everywhere.

"Maybe they want to open a deli to compete with Murray. If you are going to go against the competition, what better way than to get the competition's most popular item on your own menu. This way they get part of Murray's profits and get to make money from selling his delicious knishes," said Rachel.

"I just can't see the mob looking to get into the kosher deli business."

"I don't know, but if anyone can figure it out and help Murray it's you. Who knows? Maybe you will get Tony the Tilapia to lain tefilin by the time you are done with this."

"It might happen. However, he would have to change his name to Tony the Gefilte Fish."

Chapter 3

Saturday morning's Shabbat service was particularly busy since it was Levi Rubinstein's bar mitzvah. Levi did a wonderful job with his Haftorah and gave a heartfelt speech thanking just about everyone in the temple. Levi's family sponsored a kiddush for him after the service.

While at the kiddush I decided to talk to one of my good friends, Eytan Barak, a former Israeli Mossad agent turned accountant of all things. Despite that he now balanced ledger sheets, as opposed to infiltrating Arab terrorist groups, Eytan had connections everywhere and had lots of friends in the FBI and CIA. I suspected that he still did some covert work, but he would never confirm or deny this. Eytan also helped me now and then when I needed back up. Having Eytan around was equivalent to having three guys as back up. I figured Eytan might be able to point me in a direction with regard to Murray's knish problem.

"Eytan, can I talk to you for a moment?" I asked.

"Of course Rabbi."

Eytan and I went to my office.

"Murray Goldstein has a problem. He came to see me earlier this week. Three guys in expensive Italian suits came to see Murray at his deli. Tony the Tilapia told Murray that the organization he represents wants part of Murray's profits from the deli and wants to buy knishes from him at cost."

"Tony the Tilapia works for the Balduccis. They are a criminal syndicate based out of New York. They own a lot of waterfront property in New York and New Jersey. They are in the construction business which is a front for their, shall we say, illegal businesses including drugs and running numbers. They also do loan sharking for exceedingly high interest rates."

"Did you learn all of this doing quarterly statements for your clients?" I asked.

"You would be amazed what you can learn from preparing quarterly statements and annual reports," said Eytan with a smirk on his face.

"Eytan, you still work for the Mossad, FBI, CIA or some other government agency with a three letter acronym, don't you?" I asked.

"I can neither confirm nor deny that."

"Do you practice saying that in your sleep?" I asked.

"I can neither confirm nor deny that," said Eytan.

"What a kidder you are. Fine. Don't tell me. It is not like I'm your Rabbi. Not to worry."

"Rabbi, your guilt does not work on me. As a Mossad agent I am impervious to guilt."

"So you are still a Mossad agent. I knew it!!" I exclaimed.

"I did not say that Rabbi. I said as a Mossad agent. Even if I am no longer working with the Mossad, which I can neither confirm nor deny, I will always consider myself an agent of the Mossad."

"You should have been a lawyer Eytan. So who can I talk to about the Balduccis's operations? Murray is really scared."

"I know a guy who may have some information. He works for the government," said Eytan.

"Just like you do," I said.

"I can neither confirm nor deny that statement. His name is Brian Thompson. I will tell him to give you a call."

Chapter 4

Brian Thompson, who works in the FBI's Miami Field Office, gave me a call on Tuesday. We arranged to meet for coffee at a restaurant on 30th and Collins Avenue. I got there early and got a booth. I was able to spot Agent Thompson as soon as he walked in. He was wearing the typical government employee dark suit and black shoes. Government employees have a certain look about them which I could spot after ten years as a cop. Since I had a beard and a yarmulke, Agent Thompson was able to spot me when he walked in the door. I guess rabbis have a certain look as well.

"Hi," said Agent Thompson. "You must be Rabbi Klein."

"The one and not only," I said.

"I would be willing to bet there is more than one Rabbi Klein."

"You're right. My father and brothers for starters.

There could be a few others floating around."

"What can I do for you Rabbi?"

"One of my congregants owns a very popular Jewish deli in town. He has the rightful claim to possibly having the best knishes in the South Florida area."

"Eytan filled me in on some of the details of what your congregant is dealing with, but he left out one important part. What is a knish?"

"A knish is a Jewish delicacy. Knishes have a flaky pastry texture on the outside and are filled with different items such as potato or kasha."

"What is kasha?"

"Agent Thompson, did you think when you woke up this morning you would be getting a lesson on Jewish food?"

"I learn something new everyday."

"That makes two of us. Kasha is barley or buckwheat and is often served with bow tie pasta. One of my most favorite dishes."

"Sounds delightful. From what I understand, your congregant was visited by three individuals of Italian descent who are named after various fishes."

"That's correct. Eytan said the three men work for

the Balduccis out of New York."

We keep a close eye on the Balduccis, but they are quite good at covering their tracks, burying those they take care of in hard to find graves and moving their products around so that government agencies don't see it happen."

"Smart, well-thought out organized criminals. Who knew?"

"The government has cracked down pretty hard on the mafia over the last twenty years. For the crime families to survive, they had to get smarter in their operations. Gone are the days when they could flaunt what they were doing and not be prosecuted."

"What are the names of the guys who paid your congregant a visit?"

"Tony the Tilapia, Sammy the Salmon and Guido the Grouper."

"All fine upstanding citizens if you take away the drug dealing, running numbers and murder."

"We all have our faults," I said.

"What did Tony want with your congregant?"

"Tony said that some people he works for are also in the knish business on a large scale. They want to buy knishes from Murray at cost and want part of his profits."

"Wanting part of the profits is the easy part. If Tony sees a profitable business he wants part of the action.

The part I don't get is why he wants to buy knishes at cost from your congregant."

"Neither do I. I was hoping you may have a way to find out," I said.

"The Balduccis own some restaurants and food distribution businesses. They deal in fish and steak. It would be unusual for the Balduccis, or crime families in general, to get involved with ethnic food products they know nothing about. Crime families are not looking to learn about food. They want to sell what they know and make money doing it. They don't necessarily know the market for selling to Jewish delis and would likely have difficulty convincing delis to buy from them."

"That is true. Jewish delis buy their products from distributors they are familiar with in order to insure the products are prepared according to certain kosher standards," I said.

"If the Balduccis want in they have an angle. The question is what is their real interest? Let me check around a bit to see what I can find out. Eytan told me about you. He said you are a trustworthy guy. If Eytan says that, I believe it."

"Well I am honored Eytan speaks highly of me. So tell me Agent Thompson, is Eytan still working for the Mossad or some agency of the U.S. Government?"

"I can neither confirm nor deny that," said Agent Thompson.

"I am hearing that a lot lately,"I said.

Agent Thompson told me he would be in touch, got up from the booth and left.

Chapter 5

I left the restaurant and headed to the office. I had a meeting that morning with the chair of the temple board to discuss our capital campaign to build additional classrooms for the Hebrew day school. When I walked into my office, an expensively dressed woman was sitting in a chair in the reception area. Either Lola had a rich friend waiting to go to lunch with her, or someone was waiting to see me.

"Hi. I'm Rabbi Klein. Can I help you?" I asked.

"Yes. My name is Sheila Bronstein of the Long Island Bronsteins."

"As if there could be any others," I said. "Please, step into my office."

We walked into my office. I offered Mrs. Bronstein a chair.

"Our family goes back several generations in New

York. We made our money in the garment business. We still own several factories in New York. My husband Joseph and I moved to Miami some years ago. Joseph started an import/export business. He does a lot of shipping to the Caribbean islands."

"Well, people in the islands need things shipped to them like the rest of us." I was not sure where this conversation was going, but I was pretty sure Mrs. Bronstein was going to spend some more time impressing me with her family's credentials.

"Joseph and I have two children. Todd who is sixteen and Samantha who is fourteen. They both attend Pine Ridge School in Miami. It is one of the finest private schools in the State. Tuition is $25,000 a year per child."

"You don't say. I think my temple's school is grossly undercharging. I will bring that up at our next board meeting."

"Rabbi, let me get to the point. Todd is a junior. He scored a 1440 on his SAT's. Todd wants to go to an Ivy League School, either Harvard, Yale, Princeton or Stanford. He has the grades and extra curricular activities to get there."

"You should be quite proud Mrs. Bronstein. Todd sounds like a good boy."

"Well, that's what brings me here. Lately Todd hasbeen hanging around with a group of kids who have gotten into some trouble."

"Boys will be boys. It happens. Nothing too serious I hope?"I asked.

"I don't know for sure. Todd won't tell me."

"Have you spoken with the school?"

"Todd has not been caught doing anything wrong yet. However, if he keeps hanging around with this crowd, I know he will get into trouble and it may impact his ability to get into an Ivy League School. I can't allow that to happen."

"What would you like me to do Mrs. Bronstein?"

"Talk to Todd. See what you can find out. Speak with someone at the school. Find out about the kids Todd is hanging around with."

"My fee is $100 per hour plus expenses. My initial retainer is $600."

"Money is no object Rabbi."

"To the contrary, money is an object, rectangular in shape and flat but very useful."

Despite her serious demeanor, my witty comment caused Mrs. Bronstein to smirk.

"Good point Rabbi. Please keep me informed of what you learn."

"Of course."

Chapter 6

I made an appointment to meet with the principal of Todd Bronstein's school on Wednesday afternoon. Joseph Stein's bar mitzvah was Saturday so I also had a meeting with Joseph and his mother that afternoon to go over the speech he would give after his haftorah. For years I had been waiting for the right moment during a bar or bat mitzvah to say right after the haftorah: "You only did a half torah? Why not a whole torah? You may only be half a bar or bat mitzvah." Maybe Joseph would be the lucky one.

The week before any bar or bat mitzvah was always a special time because it was the end of the year long journey of learning the haftorah and prayers and the entry of the boy or girl into Jewish adulthood. Watching them practice their speech I could see how excited they were since they were almost at the finish line, and truth be told, they knew there would be a big party and lots of presents.

I arrived at Todd's school at 2:00 PM. Pine Ridge was an amazing campus that seemed to go on for miles. It was clear from looking at the buildings why they were charging $25,000 a year. The electric bill alone for the school must be a number with many zeros behind it. I walked into the office and told the person at the front desk that I had an appointment with Principal Simmons. After waiting a few minutes I was shown into Principal Simmons's office.

"Good afternoon Rabbi."

"It's a pleasure to meet you Principal Simmons. Thank you for agreeing to meet with me regarding Todd Bronstein."

"I am always happy to do what I can to help our students. Todd is a fine student. He has good grades and comes from a good family."

"Todd's mother tells me that he has fallen in with some troublesome kids lately and she is concerned. She hired me to find out what Todd is up to and to help prevent him from affecting his chances of going to an Ivy League school."

"Forgive me for asking, but why did Todd's mother hire a Rabbi to find this out?"

"Good question. I am also a private investigator.

I am working on a joke involving a Rabbi, a priest, a private investigator and a monkey walking into a bar since I can play two roles in the joke."

Principal Simmons laughed at my joke that was not quite a joke yet.

"Well, you are the first Rabbi/private investigator I have ever met."

"I get that a lot. I am looking into a bumper sticker or a t-shirt proclaiming me as the one and only Rabbi/private investigator so I can corner the market."

"I think Todd's parents may be pushing him a bit too hard and he is rebelling. It is not easy for kids today with all of their activities and the pressure to do well in school so they can get into a good college. With a successful family like Todd's, the pressure is enormous."

"I am sure that it is. Being that Pine Ridge is such a prestigious school, I would think that getting into a good college is not a difficult task for your students, assuming their grades and SAT scores are good."

"That is true to a degree. However, there are so many students applying for spots at top schools and not all of them can get in. It is more than grades at this point. Colleges are looking for what else is on an applicant's resume. What activities are you involved in? What charities do you work with? What awards have you won? It is more like a job interview than a college application. The competition is fierce and it can be overwhelming."

"Do you know who the kids are that Todd is hanging around who are causing his parents concern?"

"I know a few of them. Something you should understand Rabbi is that even though the kids in our school come from wealthy families, it does not mean they don't get into trouble. The fact is they sometimes get into worse trouble than kids who don't have the same financial means because these kids feel a sense of privilege or entitlement and think that no one can touch them since mom and dad will get them out of anything. These kids, in a sense, rebel against their comfortable lives by doing bad things."

"I understand. I see it sometimes with kids in my congregation."

"I can give you the names of some of the kids Todd is hanging around with. I hope you understand that school policy prohibits me from giving you any other information about them."

"Names will be fine. I will put my private investigator yarmulke on to find out what else I need."

I thanked Principal Simmons, left Todd's school and headed back to my office. Lola gave me a few messages. I sat down at my desk to do some digging on the kids Todd was hanging around with. Since I was a private investigator, I had access to certain on-line databases that were only available to law enforcement and law firms. The searches I could do on these kids would be a good starting point for their backgrounds. I also learned in the last few years that Facebook can be a useful tool for gathering information.

The temple had a page on Facebook of which most of our congregation was friends, including the kids in our congregation. Since kids often became friends with other kids on Facebook who do not attend their own school, I figured I could trace my way to the kids Todd was hanging around with by looking through the friends of the kids in our congregation. Some people allowed their Facebook pages to be displayed to persons they were not friends with, so I also checked if those kids had privacy protections on their pages. After about an hour, I had some information on Todd's troublesome crowd.

Chapter 7

Thursday I met Eytan for lunch at Murray's deli. The Balduccis had not paid Murray a second visit, but we knew they would be back. We needed to come up with a plan for how to deal with the situation Murray was facing.

"I think I need to go to New York to dig around for information on the Balduccis. I can call some rabbis I know up there who can connect me with some people who should have information," I said.

"I'm sorry Rabbi. Were you talking? I am in knish heaven at the moment. Even though Jews don't believe in heaven, I am there."

"If the Mossad knew that all it takes for you to lose your focus is a good knish, they would have demoted you to mail room duty."

"Thankfully in Israel we don't have knishes like the ones Murray makes or I may have had a problem. Would you like me to go to New York with you?"

"Sure. Far be it from me to deny you the chance to get some New York bagels."

Murray sat down and joined us.

"Hi Rabbi. Any plan for how to deal with the Balduccis? I know they will be back and they may not be so nice the second time around."

I told Murray about my plan to go to New York to gather some information.

"Is Eytan going with you?"

"I am not leaving this table. I am going to keep eating knishes. I can't go anywhere," said Eytan.

"Eytan, you would put knishes before my safety?"

"Is it my fault your knishes are so good? I think you are to blame for my predicament. If your knishes were terrible I would not even be here."

Murray pondered Eytan's statement for a moment and appeared to conclude that Eytan's predicament was a compliment.

"Thank you again for your help Rabbi. Let me know what you find out."

Murray got up from our table and went into the kitchen. Eytan and I finished our meal, paid the bill and headed out.

Chapter 8

Friday I was busy in my office getting ready for Shabbat services, the bar mitzvah on Saturday and making travel arrangements for New York. Friday night services were nice as usual. I looked forward to getting home to my family for Shabbat dinner. We had some guests for dinner that night so Rachel had been cooking since she got home, although some of the cooking started Thursday night. I hugged Rebecca and Jacob as I walked in the door, kissed Rachel in the kitchen and got changed for dinner.

An hour later our guests began to arrive. When we were all seated I said kiddush. Rachel lit the candles with Rebecca. Rachel's chicken noodle soup was delicious as ever. Rebecca helped Rachel with serving the brisket, chicken, potatoes and salad. Dessert was assorted cakes and cookies from one of the kosher bakeries in town. We finished dinner and chatted about the goings on in everyone's week, sports, family, school, etc. Our dinner guests left around 10:30 PM Rebecca and Jacob went to their rooms. Rachel and I went to sit on the porch in the backyard. I poured each of us some wine and sat down.

"A lovely meal as always my dear."

"Why thank you. Your mother-in-law would be happy to hear that she did a good job teaching your wife how to cook."

"That she did. Remind me to thank her next time I see her," I said.

I told Rachel that I was going to New York to look into the situation with the Balduccis. She asked if Eytan was joining me. I told her that Eytan was at Murray's in knish heaven and assuming he returned to earth he would go with me. Rachel pointed out that Jews do not believe in heaven, to which I responded that Murray's knishes apparently transcend our Jewish beliefs and created some form of an after life which Eytan is convinced must exist. After she laughed, I told Rachel that Eytan would be going with me in case I needed any tax information for my investigation into the Balduccis. She laughed at that too. Rachel knew that Eytan would have my back, which she liked. Being a Jewish woman, worrying comes naturally to her.

I woke up early the next morning for temple

and Joseph Stein's big day. Joseph and his family arrived at the temple early, before the majority of the congregation arrived. Joseph sat on the stage waiting to be called to do his haftorah. At 10:30 AM I called Joseph to the bimah, told him that he would do great and to do it just like we had practiced. I sat down and watched as he ran through the opening prayers and then did his haftorah perfectly. There was always a moment after a bar or bat mitzvah sings the last of the prayers at the end of their haftorah when they realize they survived, they did a good job and that they are almost at the finish line. Usually they smile and have a look of relief on their faces as they sing the last line: "baruch atah adonai, mekadesh hashabat." They usually hold the "hashabat" for a bit to let the moment linger as they say to themselves: "Wow. I am done." It is always a special moment for me having gone through the year long journey to Jewish adulthood with them.

After finishing his haftorah, Joseph gave his speech. He talked about what he had learned over the last year, the charity he worked with and his plans to travel to Israel. Joseph then thanked just about everyone in the synagogue. All good things must come to an end though, which included Joseph's speech. I thanked Joseph, congratulated him on doing a wonderful job, then called up to the bimah two members of our temple's USY group to present Joseph with a membership so he could continue his involvement in the Jewish community as he moved into high school the following year.

Joseph's family sponsored a nice kiddush after the service to which everyone at the synagogue was invited. Everyone ate, drank and had a nice time while congratulating the bar mitzvah boy. At about 12:45 PM the kiddush started to wind down. Joseph's family said goodbye. I told them I would see them later that night at Joseph's party. From the details I was given, it sounded like it would be quite the party.

I went home after the kiddush and spent some time playing catch with Jacob. Joseph's bar mitzvah made me realize how quickly my children were growing up. It was over a year ago that Jacob had his bar mitzvah and Rachel would have her bat mitzvah in seven months. I decided I was a lucky man, even though I did not think Jacob had much hope of an NFL career. Baseball, maybe, or an accountant. I was pulling for baseball.

We rested a bit that afternoon and then got ready for Joseph's bar mitzvah party. Bar mitzvah parties these days were not parties—they were events. The parties had become so elaborate, so expensive and so over the top, it seemed the goal at times was to outdo the parties of those who came before you. The parties certainly diminished the true meaning of a bar or bat mitzvah, but as Bob Dylan once said: "The times they are a-changin". Whether I liked it or not, I had to change with the times as well.

We arrived at the synagogue at 8 PM. There was a red carpet out front. Red velvet ropes were on either side of the carpet. All of the guests were lined up behind the ropes waiting for Joseph to arrive. Joseph picked Hollywood and the movies as his theme. There were six photographers who were the paparazzi ready to take Joseph's picture as he arrived. About two minutes later, a limousine pulled up and Joseph was escorted out by two models on his arm who walked him up the red carpet. The crowed cheered. Light bulbs from the cameras flashed. The MC for the event, who was the singer for the band, announced Joseph's arrival with a wireless microphone and invited everyone to join the party inside. We all followed Joseph and his model escorts up the stairs into the ballroom. The ballroom was decorated with images from movies. People were dressed up as famous actors and actresses. The stage was made to look like a scene from one of the Harry Potter movies.

The band played to welcome Joseph into the room. His escorts lead him to the dance floor where he danced with the two women. Being that Jews are not a rhythmically inclined people, since our dancing skills at events are usually limited to running in circles in either direction for Hava Nagila, or lifting people up in chairs, Joseph did the best he could to keep up. I always thought that being the Chosen People would have come with rhythm as a skill. Alas, it was not true.

We all found our seats so the party could begin. We were then told to get on the dance floor to dance with the bar mitzvah boy. We formed a large circle and started to do the hora. Joseph's friends formed a smaller circle within the large circle to dance with him. Then, some of Joseph's relatives formed a smaller circle to dance with him. Next, Joseph danced with his father, arm in arm, in both directions in a circle. Then, Joseph's mother and some of his other female relatives formed a circle around him, rushing right up to him, then back out again. After ten or so minutes, the last notes were played and we were told to find our seats. The salads were then served. Rachel and I chatted with the people at our table who were members of the synagogue. We were caught up on how kids were doing in school, sports, jobs and other activities. We spoke about recent events in Israel involving yet another bombing that killed ten people.

Dinner was then served. Once we finished, it was time for the candle lighting ceremony. Relatives, groups of friends and teachers (including myself) were all called up to light a candle. It seemed like everyone except for Joseph's two model escorts got to light a candle. After the candle lighting ceremony, the band played a few slow songs. Rachel and I danced. The kids at the party who were at the age where they were interested in the opposite sex, but did not want to slow dance with each other, avoided the dance floor. Once the band started playing songs the kids knew, they hit the dance floor to show us older folks how it is done. Based on the moves I saw, I decided to leave the dancing up to the kids.

The party finished around 1:00 AM. We said our goodbyes, thanked Joseph's parents, congratulated Joseph and headed home. Jacob and Rebecca slept the whole drive to the house. Apparently dancing is a tiresome activity.

Chapter 9

Tuesday morning Eytan and I were on a flight to New York. Eytan insisted on an aisle seat since if someone tried to commit an act of terrorism aboard the flight he did not want to have to ask one or two people to step out of the way so he could beat a terrorist's head in. I decided that was a reasonable request so I took the window seat. Due to Eytan's intention to keep our flight safe, he did not sleep and instead read a book. While appearing intensely engrossed in his book, I knew that Eytan was aware of everything going on around him. If anything seemed out of place, or anyone did something out of the ordinary, Eytan would be on them before they could get very far into their plan. Although I did not expect anything to happen, it was nice knowing that Eytan was there just in case.

We landed at JFK at 10:30 AM, got a cab and headed into the city. Before business came lunch and we were not going to pass up the opportunity to visit one of the numerous Jewish delis in the city. I ordered corned beef on rye with mustard and lettuce, and in honor of the purpose of our trip, a knish. Eytan went with the roast beef on rye and voted against a knish since he believed there was no finer knish than those he got at Murray's deli, so any other knish would just lead to disappointment. I explained to Eytan that his knish view was rather extreme, to which he replied that one must have standards.

After lunch we checked into our hotel. After we got settled into our room, we headed back out to meet with Rabbi Yossi Steinberg who is the Rabbi for a temple located on the upper west side. Yossi and I went to rabbinical school together and had kept in touch over the years. Yossi is very well connected in the community and has several police officers who are members of his congregation.

We got out of the cab and walked through the entrance of the temple. The receptionist told us to have a seat and that Yossi would be with us in a moment. Yossi came out a few minutes later with his usual cheerful smile on his face.

"Moshe, it's been what, three years? How are you my friend?"

"I'm doing well Yossi. You look good. Rivkah still taking good care of you?"

"I am a lucky man Moshe. She puts up with me which is not so easy."

"If it was easy they would not say that marriage is hard work. She's lucky to have you."

"I know. I keep reminding her of that. Sometimes she manages not to roll her eyes when I say it."

Eytan laughed. I introduced him to Yossi. I told Yossi that Eytan was my accountant. Yossi asked why I travel with my accountant. I told Yossi that Eytan used to be in the Mossad and may still be, which he would neither confirm nor deny. Yossi told me someone who could do my taxes while defending me against a physical attack was indeed a good person with whom to travel.

"Moshe," said Yossi, "I spoke to a few of my congregants who are police officers and they set up a meeting for you with someone in NYPD's organized crime unit. Based on what you told me your friend Murray is dealing with, they may have some information on the Balduccis which will help you. I have the address of the police station for you. Ask for Sergeant Michael O'Leary. He is expecting you in forty-five minutes."

We thanked Yossi and said our goodbyes. Eytan and I caught a cab to the police station. When we arrived we were directed to the third floor. We took the stairs and found the office. We told the desk officer that we were there to see Sergeant O'Leary. We waited a minute and then Sergeant O'Leary came out of his office. He was a large man who clearly worked out a lot and may have had a sports career before going into police work. If I had to guess, he played linebacker somewhere before getting his badge.

"You must be Rabbi Klein. I'm Sergeant O'Leary."

"Nice to meet you Sergeant. This is Eytan. He keeps me out of trouble."

Sergeant O'Leary took a look at Eytan and said he suspected Eytan had seen some trouble in his day. Eytan said he could neither confirm nor deny that. After I told the Sergeant that Eytan was at one time in the Mossad, Sergeant O'Leary gave a nod of approval and showed us to his office. In his office I saw some pictures of a younger Sergeant wearing an Ohio State uniform.

"So you played ball in college?" I asked.

"I did. Linebacker. I had a chance to go pro, but got injured in my senior year. So, I decided to become a cop."

"Me too."

"You played ball?"

"I did. I blew out my knee in my senior year. I became a cop first. I worked ten years with Miami PD, and then went on to become a Rabbi."

"So there is still hope that I can become a Rabbi?" asked Sergeant O'Leary.

"If you are willing to change your last name to O'Learybergstein, I will see what I can do."

"I think my mother would have a problem with me doing that. I guess I will stick with the cop thing. So, I understand a friend of yours is having an issue with the Balduccis?"

"Yes he is. Murray Goldstein runs a popular deli in Miami Beach. Murray is known for having some of the best knishes in South Florida."

"Despite that my last name does not end with Bergstein, I actually know what a knish is and am a fan of them myself."

"Well, we may not be able to make a Rabbi out of you, but we may be able to make a good Jew out of you Sergeant."

"That would also not go over well with my Irish Catholic mother. I will let you explain that one to her."

"I think I will let Eytan do that instead. He does well with mothers."

"So what do the Balduccis want from your friend Murray?" O'Leary asked.

"Three of the Balduccis named after fishes came to visit Murray recently and told him they are involved in the knish business on a large scale. They want a percentage of his profits and want Murray to sell them large quantities of knishes at cost."

"Interesting. To our knowledge, the Balduccis do not have a presence in South Florida. That would be new territory for them. They are involved in the seafood and steak business in New York, New Jersey and Philadelphia. Knishes do not make any sense. The Balduccis are one of the most powerful crime families in the northeast. They have their hands in lots of illegal activities including prostitution, drugs, loan sharking, and the protection racket. It does not seem that buying knishes at cost from your friend Murray, even in large quantities, is going to give the Balduccis a high profit margin business since they would need a buyer, and crime families like the Balduccis don't make their money in specialized or niche markets foods. They are up to something. We have tried to make something stick on them for a while, but they are quite good at covering their tracks. They are visible with their legitimate businesses and quite good at hiding the non-legitimate ones."

"That is the million shekel question Sergeant."

"Well, I don't know the exact currency exchange rate, but I do know one million shekels is nowhere near a million dollars. It is more like the $250,000 question."

"Look at this guy Eytan. There really is hope for him becoming a Jew."

Eytan and Sergeant O'Leary laughed.

"Tell you what Rabbi. Let me dig around to see if I can find out why the Balduccis are interested in your friend."

"We appreciate it. Murray is a good man and he is quite scared about this situation. He is also quite stubborn and he is not going to agree to the Balduccis's demand which could lead to trouble."

"Knowing the Balduccis it will lead to very big trouble for your friend Murray. The Balduccis get what they want one way or another. They have offered your friend Murray the easy way. Soon they will come back offering him the not so easy way."

"That's what we are counting on Sergeant."

Eytan smiled. I suspected his smile had nothing to do with preparing tax returns.

Chapter 10

Eytan and I caught an early afternoon Yankees game on Wednesday and headed to the airport to catch an evening flight back to Miami. I again conceded the aisle seat to Eytan for my own safety and that of my fellow passengers. I read a book and spent part of the flight thinking about what to do with Murray and the Balduccis. I was forming a plan. I would need help and Eytan would know who to call.

I got back to my house around 11:30 PM. The kids were asleep and so was Rachel. I quietly walked into the bedroom hoping I would not wake her. When I got into bed she stirred a bit.

"How was New York?" she asked.

"Eytan took the aisle seat."

"He likes to protect the passengers. I like that about him."

"Me too."

"Tell me more in the morning."

"I will. Get some rest."

Rachel drifted back to sleep. Within a few minutes I was also asleep.

I got up early the next morning and made breakfast for my family. Rachel was quite impressed when she came downstairs and saw the table set, food on the table, juice poured and coffee brewed. The kids came downstairs a few minutes later and were similarly impressed. I briefly considered how my business card would look with the titles, "Rabbi, private investigator and chef", and concluded I would need to spend significant time improving my cooking skills before putting "chef" on my business card. There are only so many omelettes and pieces of French toast one can eat, and aside from those two dishes, my cooking skills were limited to some basic pasta, fish and chicken items. My rise to chef status would have to wait.

I served everyone some food, poured Rachel and I some coffee, and sat down to tell Rachel about my trip with Eytan. The kids half listened in between texting their friends and reviewing notes for quizzes they had that morning. I told Rachel about our meeting with Sergeant O'Leary and his being baffled by what the Balduccis would want with Murray's knishes. Rachel asked if I had a plan. I told her I was working on one.

Rachel and I reached an agreement years ago that as to matters in my private investigation life at times there would be danger so she would not ask too many questions to avoid excessive worrying. As a Jewish mother worrying was built into her DNA, so I did not need to add to her worries. Two teenage kids and a husband who did private investigation work was enough to worry about without having the details of my work to contend with. Knowing that Eytan would be involved with me in whatever plan I came up with gave her enough relief that she could go about her day.

After breakfast I said goodbye to Rachel, got the kids in the car and dropped them off at school. I headed to my office to check in with Lola to see what I missed while in New York. While in the car I called Murray and asked him to meet me at the office so I could give him an update. I thought it best I get to my office before Murray arrived because if he and Lola were left alone I might walk into a boxing match which I suspected Murray would be losing.

I walked into the office, said "shalom" to Lola and filled her in on the details of my trip. She asked if I had a plan, to which I responded I was working on one. I then told Lola that Murray was stopping by for an update. She rolled her eyes and mumbled under her breath that Murray better not start any trouble with her or else. Murray came into the office a few minutes later, said hello to Lola, handed her a paper bag and took a step back. Lola opened the bag, saw it was a bagel and lox, gave Murray a suspicious look, and then decided to accept his peace offering. She thanked Murray and told him he could go see me in my office.

"Good morning Rabbi," said Murray with a big smile on his face.

"Way to go with the peace offering Murray. You apparently know the way to Lola's heart and it is through her stomach when it comes to food from your deli."

"I have my gifts. So tell me about New York."

I filled Murray in on the details of the trip.

"Do you have a plan?" asked Murray.

I noted that I was getting that question a lot lately. I concluded I better have one heck of a plan or many people would be disappointed.

"I do have a plan. I expect the Balduccis will contact you again soon. When they do, tell them if they want in on your business they need to meet with your business partners."

"But Rabbi, I don't have any business partners."

I leaned back in my chair, put my hands behind my head and smiled.

"You do now."

Chapter 11

I told Murray the details of phase one of my plan. He seemed pleased, thanked me, and headed back to the deli. I asked Lola what I had on my calendar for the day. I had a meeting at 5 PM to discuss the synagogue's annual Purim festival. I took care of some paperwork and met Eytan for lunch to discuss my plan. I told Eytan that my plan would require assistance from a few of his associates who were also former, or possibly current Mossad agents, since I assumed they all had the same "I can neither confirm nor deny" answer when asked if they were still involved with the Mossad. Eytan said that he had some people he could call who would be happy to help. According to Eytan, current and former Mossad agents would go to great lengths to protect Miami Beach's best Jewish deli with legendary knishes. I told Eytan I admired their commitment.

I left the restaurant and headed back to my office. I called Agent Thompson and gave him an update on the situation with Murray and the Balduccis. I told him I was working on a plan and that we should meet since I would like his help. He said he was available Thursday morning. We agreed to meet for coffee.

Lola came into my office. She sat down looking troubled.

"Something wrong Lola?"I asked.

"Yes. Cindy is at that age where I have to have the talk."

"You are going to talk to her about converting to Judaism so she can have a bat mitzvah? She is twelve so the clock is ticking."

"How did I get so lucky to work for the one Rabbi who is a private investigator and thinks he is a comedian?"

"By Hashem himself Lola you are blessed."

"Blessings come in many forms. Some, not so blessful."

"I think you are making up words Lola."

"I'm Italian. I can do that."

"Fair point."

"So, since your daughter will not be lucky enough to be converting to Judaism, the talk must be don't do drugs, don't drink until you are twenty one and don't have sex ever."

"Ever would be good, but not realistic."

"Seems it is not. The world would be far less populated if ever was realistic."

"But that would contradict the directive of the Lord that thou shalt be fruitful and multiply."

"Very true," I said.

"Any helpful rabbinical tips for how I can approach the subject with Cindy?"

"I do have some, but they go beyond just the talk. You can give the greatest talk in the world, but if you don't keep your eyes wide open for signs of trouble, or things Cindy is doing that you don't want her to do, your talk will do little good. Cindy needs to know that if there are issues she can come to you and not be judged. You may not always like what you hear, but an open line of communication is imperative. Cindy will be pressured by her friends to do certain things. The more productive of a talk you have with her, the better chance she won't do things you don't want her to do, or at least not too many things. The reality is you can only do so much. At some point it is up to Cindy to make her own choices, even if they are bad ones. Like birds in the nest, we do our best for eighteen years and then send them off to fly on their own and hope they don't got shot at or crash into too many trees."

"May I ask what you have told your kids?"

"I told them if they drink, do drugs or have sex, their grandmother will find out and answering to her is worse than answering to me or Rachel. They know this to be true. However, I am realistic. They may do something I don't want them to do. Thus, when I spoke to them about sex I told them it would be best if they wait until they are over eighteen and to do it with someone they love. Regardless, I told them they must always use protection. I then had them watch twelve hours of 'Teen Mom' on MTV. I think that did the trick."

"And what about drinking?"

"I told them that some of their friends will drink, and they will be at parties where other kids will pressure them to drink. They have to make a choice. It is o.k. to say no. They can volunteer to be the designated driver if any of their friends drink. Everyone loves the designated driver. That way, they don't have to worry about being made fun of. They also know that if they should ever drink they are never to drive home and they are not to get into the car with any of their friends who have been drinking. Instead, they are to call me and I will pick them up a few blocks away from wherever they are so their friends don't see their uncool Rabbi father picking them up."

"Do you really think they would call you if they were drinking and could not drive home?"

"They know that there will not be any judgment of their actions if they do call, at least not at that time. A student in their school died while driving home from a party because he had been drinking. He crashed into a tree and was killed on impact. They understand the importance of calling me. All I can do is hope that they will do the right thing."

"Cindy is a smart kid. I think she will make the right decisions, but I still worry."

"You are supposed to worry Lola. After all, you are an honorary Jewish mother."

Chapter 12

At 5 PM I headed to the conference room for the Purim festival committee meeting. The meeting was relatively peaceful. We had two co-chairs who both had some good ideas. We needed to have a good balance of activities so that the festival would appeal to both the adults and the children of the congregation. We wrapped up the meeting with a list of deadlines and agreed to meet again in a few weeks.

Jacob had a basketball game that night. He plays in a local league and is pretty good. I got there just as the game was starting. By halftime Jacob's team was up by 12 points. Jacob sat out part of the third period and played most of the fourth. His team won by 15 points. I took him out for pizza at one of the local kosher pizza places to celebrate his victory. We spoke about school and how he was doing in his classes. He gave me an update on some of his friends, and then we discussed what we thought of the Heat's chances to win a championship this year with the trades they made during the off-season.

When I got home, I said hello to Rachel and Rebecca. My cell phone rang. It was Murray. I went into the backyard to take the call.

"Hi Rabbi. The Balduccis called. They want to meet. I told them Thursday at 10 PM after the deli is closed."

"Did you tell them you were inviting your business partners?"

"I did. They did not seem pleased."

"Good. Your business partners and I will be ready."

I hung up with Murray. We knew the Balduccis would be calling soon so I told Murray to agree to schedule the meeting for two days after they called since I knew Eytan and his friends could be ready on two days notice. I called Eytan and told him the meeting was set. He said he would take care of things on his end. We would be at Murray's deli at 9 PM just in case the Balduccis showed up early to stir up some trouble while customers were still around.

I walked back into the house and looked at Rachel. I thought about telling her that I would be meeting with the Balduccis, but it would just worry her. I decided to stick with our understanding that my work was sometimes dangerous and that she was o.k. with me not filling her in on all of the details.

Chapter 13

I met Agent Thompson for coffee on Thursday morning. I told him about my plan for the Balduccis.

"Your plan is rather bold and likely very dangerous. The Balduccis won't take kindly to your involvement in this. They may take it out on your friend Murray."

"Danger is my Hebrew middle name."

"A Rabbi and a comedian, who knew?"

"I get that a lot."

"Do you also get told to keep your day job?"

"I get that a lot too. It comes right after the comedian part."

"Well, I work for the government and we have no sense of humor."

"I think I read that in Esquire Magazine, or maybe saw it on CNN."

"Rabbi, we would love to nail the Balduccis and break up their operations. If you think you can get something of substance that we can stick on them, let me know and I will see what I can do to help."

"I appreciate it."

Agent Thompson and I finished our coffee. I then left the restaurant and headed to my office.

I had a wedding on Saturday and the rehearsal was that afternoon. Frank and Jennifer were a nice young couple who met at our temple. Frank was a lawyer and Jennifer was a teacher. They had been dating for three years. They were having a large wedding with three hundred guests. At 4 PM, Frank, Jennifer and the other people in their wedding party arrived for the rehearsal. The proud parents of the bride and groom were also there. Frank's four year old cousin Michael who was the ring bearer was not in attendance.

Over the years I had learned that being the ring bearer is traumatic enough for young children who sometimes cry their way down the aisle, or get stage fright last minute and refuse to go down the aisle. Thus, I do not think making the ring bearer rehearse is a good idea since it may give them a few days to think about and plan their refusal to participate in the wedding ceremony. The hope was that without much time to think they would just do as they were asked and forgo the crying.

After some chatting I put everyone in their places. The music played and the bridesmaids were escorted down the aisle by the groomsmen. Everyone smiled and walked at the right pace to space themselves out. They lined up on the bimah and waited for the bride to be. Frank's parents walked him down the aisle. Then, Jennifer came in with her parents on either side of her escorting her down the aisle. We could all see that she was blushing imagining herself walking down the aisle for real in a few days. She walked up onto the bimah. Frank took her hand and they stood there together, soon to be man and wife.

I gave my opening remarks. We went through the prayers. We then got to the all important moment.

"Frank, do you take Jennifer to be your lawfully wedded wife, to have and to hold, to love and cherish, in sickness and health until death do you part?"

Frank looked at Jennifer, said "I . . . " and hesitated. He then got a terrified look on his face, looked quite pale, turned around and ran out of the synagogue. Jennifer started crying hysterically. Her parents ran up to the bimah to comfort her, as did her bridesmaids. The groomsmen looked around not sure of what they were supposed to do. Frank's parents were not sure if they should comfort Jennifer as well and tell her everything would be o.k., or go find Frank. Since this was not my first wedding I told everyone to relax and that I would go find Frank.

I checked a few rooms and eventually found Frank in the library reading a rabbinical text.

"Frank. Want to talk?"

"Rabbi, I don't know that I can go through with this."

"Why not Frank?"

"I do means forever. Forever is a long time. A really long time."

"If you do it right, yes it is. Forever with the right person is a good thing. You should be so lucky."

"I know, but what if it does not work? What if she is not the right person? What if I am not the right person? What if I can't give her what she wants and make her happy?"

"All good questions Frank. Let me ask you a question. Why did you decide you wanted to marry Jennifer?"

"Well, she is my best friend. She understands me. She respects me. We have fun together. I enjoy being with her. I am a better person with her in my life. She is funny. She loves kids. She likes college football and watches it with me. Do you know how tough it is to find a woman who will watch an entire season of college football with you?"

"Yes I do. That is one of the reasons I married Rachel."

"How do you make it work Rabbi? Marriage is not easy."

"That is true. If it was easy the divorce rate would not be so high. It is hard work Frank. Very hard work. Some days are better than others. Some days you will get along great. Some days you won't like each other much. What matters is that you work at it and how you work through the tough times. They will happen. Make no mistake. But I know that you and Jennifer will do it because you love each other and want to be together."

"I do want to be with her. I am lucky to have her. Her parents even like me. How often do parents like the person their child marries?"

"Not very often. You are among an elite group."

"Do your in-laws like you?" asked Frank.

"Of course they do Frank. Everyone loves Rabbis. What's not to love?"

Frank laughed. That was a good sign.

"O.k. Frank. Here is what we are going to do. I am going to get you out of this little mess you created back there. If you do as I say everything will be fine. You are not the first person I have dealt with who freaked our before their wedding day. The last one ran right out the door and made it about five miles before he realized what he had done. You did not get very far which means your freak out was a small one."

"Whatever you tell me to do I will do Rabbi. I love Jennifer. I don't want her upset over this."

"She is already upset Frank. That part we can't change. What we can do is get this wedding back on track so that lovely girl in there will still want to marry you and her parents won't kill you."

"Oh boy. I am in big trouble, aren't I?"

"Somewhat, but we will fix it. Here is what we are going to do. I am going to go back into the synagogue and tell Jennifer that I found you, that you and I talked and that everything is fine. I am then going to ask Jennifer to come speak with you. We want to keep everyone else out of this since they will want answers for what happened which will not help the situation. When Jennifer comes in here you need to tell her how you feel. Do not try to explain what you did since nothing you say will make it right. She just needs to know that you love her and want to marry her. Any questions?"

"Do you really think this will work?"

"Yes. Can I trust you won't run away while I am gone?"

"I am not going anywhere Rabbi."

"Good. I'll be right back."

I walked out of the library, went back into the synagogue and surveyed the scene. Jennifer's parents were trying to console her as she was crying. The bridesmaids were also trying to help. The groomsmen were off to the side staring at the ground or the ceiling not sure what they were supposed to do except to stay out of the way. I walked up to Jennifer who had her head in her hands. She stopped crying for a minute, looked up at me and asked if I spoke to Frank. I said that I did. I asked everyone to wait in the synagogue and then asked Jennifer to come with me. We walked out of the synagogue and I told Jennifer I would take her to speak with Frank. Before we got to the library I stopped and faced her.

"Jennifer, Frank loves you. You know that. Sometimes before weddings these things happen. I have seen it many times before. You cannot take what happened as a sign that he does not want to marry you or that he is not ready. Marriage is a big step for anyone and the realization that one is about to get married manifests in people in different ways. Frank stayed in the building which is a good sign. Some people make it several miles before stopping. Nothing I can say will change what just happened in there, but I assure you he wants to marry you. Please know that if you go in there and beat up on him for what he did you will not change it and may make things worse. Listen to what he has to say and find it in your heart to forgive him. You would much prefer something like this happen three days before the wedding than on the day of your wedding."

"O.k. Rabbi. I will try."

Jennifer and I walked into the library. Frank looked up and saw Jennifer. He got up and walked over to her and took her hands.

"Jennifer, I am so sorry for what I just did. I cannot excuse it and I will not try to. That had to hurt having your friends and family see me run out like that. I never want to hurt you. I freaked out. I want to do everything I can to make you happy and I want to marry you so we can spend the rest of our lives together. I want that more than anything."

Jennifer looked at Frank and started crying again.

I knew these were good tears. Frank kissed her and they hugged.

"Now that you two are o.k., I need to go calm down the crowd in the synagogue. Here is what I want you to do. You two sit here for a minute and talk. I will go into the synagogue and tell them that everything is o.k. You two come into the synagogue in two minutes holding hands, looking like the happy soon to be married couple."

Frank and Jennifer looked at each other and smiled.

"We will."

I walked back into the synagogue. Jennifer's mother asked me if everything was o.k. I told everyone that I had good news. Ashton Kutcher decided to do a Jewish version of "Punk'd" and the whole incident with Frank running out of the synagogue was part of the show. I told everyone to take a bow and look for the cameras. Although some of them did not want to laugh, they did.

"Seriously though, everything is fine. Frank had a minor freak out moment. He and Jennifer are talking. They will be in here in a minute. Let's not focus on what happened or ask questions. Let us instead rehearse for this wedding we are all looking forward to."

Jennifer's and Frank's parents thanked me.

Everyone lined up. A minute later Frank and Jennifer came walking down the aisle holding hands and smiling. They walked onto the bimah together. We went through the rehearsal without further incident. When we were finished, I told everyone I would see them Saturday night.

My afternoon of saving a wedding had been easy compared to what my night had in store. Tonight I had to go meet Tony and his gang.

Chapter 14

I met Eytan at his house at 7:30 PM He opened the door and I followed him into the living room. In his living room were four very large former or current members of the Mossad dressed in suits. They were loading various guns which they were putting into holsters under their suits. Additional firearms were placed in the back of their pants as well as in ankle holsters. Two of the four had knives placed inside the pockets of their jackets. I was introduced to the team. Eytan had already filled them in on the details so I did not have much to add. I decided against asking whether the team was currently involved with the Mossad since I knew I would get the same answer Eytan always gave me.

After I was introduced to the team, I went to change into my suit. We then made small talk for a bit and headed to the deli at 8:30 PM so we would be there a bit before 9 PM. We took two cars just in case things got a bit hairy and one car was not enough. We parked one car in the customer parking lot and another car in an adjacent restaurant so it would not be associated with us. In case the Balduccis tried anything funny with one car, they would not get both cars.

When we walked into the deli, Murray was finishing up with the dinner crowd. He saw us walk in and gave us a big smile. I could tell he felt at ease knowing that while the Balduccis were paying him a visit tonight, he would be well protected. Murray introduced himself to everyone and thanked them for coming. We all sat in a booth and drank coffee. At 9:30 PM the last customer left and Murray locked the front door. Murray told his staff to head out early that night since he would clean up. The staff looked a bit puzzled, but Murray was the boss and they were not going to argue with getting out a bit early.

We sat for a few more minutes and heard a banging on the door.

"Hey Murray. It's Tony. Open the door."

Murray took a deep breath, walked to the door and opened it. In walked three gentlemen dressed in expensive Italian suits. Murray stepped back and stood just in front of Eytan and his four associates. I stood next to Murray.

"You must be Murray's business partners. I'm Tony

the Tilapia. This is Sammy the Salmon and Guido the Grouper."

If Tony was concerned about the size of Murray's business partners, he did not let it show.

"They call me the Rabbi. This here is Abraham, David, Isaac, Solomon and Jacob."

"Someone really likes biblical names," said Tony.

"You like names of fish. We like biblical names," I said. "Let us sit and talk business."

We all moved to a large table in the middle of the diner Murray had put together for the meeting. I sat in the middle on one side with my team. Murray purposely was seated behind us. Tony, Sammy and Guido sat on the other side with Tony in the middle.

"Tony," I said, "as you know we are Murray's business partners. We are with an outfit from Israel that operates in many areas including Miami Beach. May I ask why it is that your organization from up north is interested in moving into our territory?"

"Well Rabbi, the Balduccis are in many businesses including food. We have a large network up north in the steak and fish business. We are looking to expand our operations into some ethnic foods and Murray's knishes came highly recommended."

"And of all things to expand into you picked knishes? Forgive my surprise Tony."

"As part of our expansion we are looking to niche markets."

"And why should we cut you in on our operation Tony? We don't like to share."

"Perhaps we can come to a mutually beneficial arrangement."

"Maybe. Let me ask you a question Tony. Let's say my organization was to come to New York, go to one of your businesses and tell them we want to buy product at cost and want part of the profits. How would you react to that?"

"I would find the people who were infringing upon my territory and make sure they knew that they would greatly regret their decision if they proceeded."

"Exactly. Respect Tony. It is key. So tell me why should my organization not make clear to yours that you have disrespected us?"

Sammy's and Guido's hands moved towards the opposite side of their jackets. Eytan and his group did the same.

"Now, now Tony. That won't solve anything."

"Sammy. Guido. Relax," said Tony. "Rabbi, when

we came to talk to Murray we did not know he was involved with an organization. If we did, we would have made a different offer. Please accept my apologies. We meant no disrespect."

"Apology accepted. So what sort of business proposal do you have in mind?"

"You sell us knishes in large quantities and we will give you part of the profits."

"And where are you going to sell these knishes? Certainly not in our territory in Miami."

"No. Of course not. Up north."

"Although not ours, there are Jewish interests up north. They would need to sign off on your expanding into a niche market involving kosher food."

"As we would expect someone moving into our territory to get our approval, we will of course do the same," said Tony.

"They may want a piece of the action as well as a show of respect."

"I believe we can work something out."

"Good. We will check with our contacts up north. How can I reach you Tony?"

Tony snapped his fingers and Sammy pulled out a card and wrote a number on it. He gave the card to

Tony who handed it across the table to me.

"Call this number and leave a message. I will get back to you."

Tony, Sammy and Guido got up and walked out of Murray's deli. Murray let out a big breath as though he had not breathed since Tony and his friends walked into the deli.

"That went well," I said.

"Tony and his pals did not get hurt. Good for them," said Eytan.

"Raise your hand if you believe that Tony simply wants to branch out into the kosher niche market," I said.

I looked at Eytan, his team and Murray and no one's hand was raised.

"I don't believe it either," I said.

Now I had to figure out what Tony was up to. Good thing I was a private investigator.

Chapter 15

Eytan's team headed out in one car. Eytan and I took the other car. Eytan dropped me off at home. Rachel was sitting on the couch waiting for me.

"I could not sleep. I know I am not supposed to worry about you but I do."

"I appreciate it. Everything is fine. The meeting with the Balduccis went well. They all agreed to convert to Judaism and have bar mitzvahs. I expect they will have large and lavish parties with lots of pasta."

"Funny Moshe. What did you learn?"

"I learned that the Balduccis are not telling us the full story. I need to figure out what they are up to."

"And you will. That's what you do."

"I also take out the garbage. You put me in charge of that."

"Also true."

Rachel kissed me and walked up the stairs to bed. As I sat on the couch she stopped on the top of the stairs.

"By the way, we're going shopping on Sunday. We are getting a new couch, love seat and coffee table."

Rachel then turned around and went to the bedroom. Our living room furniture was old, but not that old. However, my wife had just sat on the couch and waited for me to come back alive from a meeting with Italian mobsters. I decided it was not a good time to tell her no. I suspected that she knew that when she told me about our upcoming shopping trip.

Chapter 16

Thankfully, Saturday's Shabbat service was peaceful. Frank's and Jennifer's wedding was Saturday night. After the drama at the rehearsal, I was hopeful the actual wedding would go off without incident.

After the Shabbat service, I went home for the afternoon to rest and to get ready for the wedding. I figured that if Frank had left town I would have heard about it, so I took the silence to be a positive sign. I probably should have suggested an ankle tracking bracelet for Frank similar to the ones they put on people under house arrest. I made a mental note to remember that the next time a bride or groom freaked out before their wedding day. I suspected Eytan knew a guy who could get me the devices at a good price.

Rachel and I got dressed and headed to the temple around 6 PM. The wedding was set to start at 8 PM. I wanted to get there early to have enough time to speak to Frank before the ceremony began to make sure he was o.k. We entered the temple and said hello to Frank's and Jennifer's parents. Jennifer was having her makeup finished. Frank was in another room with a few of the groomsmen. We were scheduled to sign the ketubah at 7:15 PM Since Frank was a lawyer, he understood the consequences of signing a contract, even one written in Hebrew which would need to be translated for him. I entered the room where Frank was waiting with his groomsmen.

"Good evening Frank and fellow groomsmen. How is everyone this evening?"

Frank had a smile on his face and looked calm. I also noticed he was not wearing running shoes.

"We are doing good Rabbi," said Frank.

I wondered whether Frank's groomsmen were put in the room to make sure he did not leave, and if he did to chase after him. If I were Jennifer's father that might have been my plan.

"Glad to hear it," I said. "Gentlemen, would you mind giving me a moment alone with Frank. I need to go over a few details with him."

Frank's groomsmen got up and left the room. I sat down across from Frank.

"It's just me and you Frank. So tell me, how are you really doing?"

"I'm fine Rabbi. Jennifer is quite forgiving which will come in handy over the next sixty or so years."

"Well, as men we tend to screw up so a forgiving wife does come in handy. I don't need to worry about you taking a stroll prior to the ceremony, correct?"

Frank laughed. "No, you don't."

"Good. You do know that Jennifer's father has connections and if you run tonight he will put a hit out on you. I don't condone it but I don't think I can stop him."

I looked at Frank with my most serious look. He looked at me with slight terror in his eyes. I paused for a moment and laughed.

"Oh Frank. You need to lighten up. Jennifer's father won't put a hit out on you. He will just break your legs himself. He is a pretty big guy you know."

"I'm not going anywhere Rabbi. You and Jennifer's father have nothing to worry about."

"That's what I wanted to hear. We will be signing the ketubah in twenty minutes."

"I look forward to it."

I got up and patted Frank on the shoulder. I walked

out of the room and told the groomsmen to keep an eye on Frank. I went to my office to get the ketubah and some pens. The signing ceremony would be in the room where the cocktail hour was to take place. I put the ketubah in the room and went to tell Frank's and Jennifer's parents to bring each of them to the room in ten minutes for the signing.

I took a quick look in the synagogue to make sure that everything was set up properly, then I went back to the room for the ketubah signing. Frank's family entered the room first. Jennifer and her family entered a minute later. Frank looked at Jennifer and had a big smile on his face. Frank took her hand and they stood together while I explained the contract into which they were about to enter. I asked if there were any questions. Frank asked where he was supposed to sign. Everyone in the room seemed to collectively breath a sigh of relief after Thursday's events. Jennifer signed next and was nearly in tears. I told her no crying until the ceremony. Tears had to be saved for the crowd, plus it would look good on the wedding video. Everyone laughed.

The families headed downstairs to take their places. Most of the guests were seated. At 8:10 PM the ceremony began. When we reached the all important question, Frank turned to Jennifer, smiled and said "I do". Jennifer smiled, held back her tears and also answered "I do". Frank stepped on the glass. I then told him he could kiss his bride. He did. Everyone clapped. Frank and Jennifer walked down the aisle with the wedding party following them.

I breathed a sigh of relief that Jennifer's father could cancel the hit he was going to take out on Frank if he messed up the "I do" part for a second time.

Chapter 17

As I was told it would be, I spent my Sunday furniture shopping. Rachel had a plan of attack. We went to an area of Miami that had several furniture stores in a row, thus how it got the nickname "Furniture Row". Rachel had done some research on-line to pick out styles she liked. She was not one to go into a situation unprepared. The couch would be leather, most likely a dark brown. The issue was what size couch she wanted. My role was limited in the search, but a pivotal one.

The first time we purchased living room furniture I explained to Rachel that I had a test I called the "couch test". I did not just sit on a couch for a few seconds like most people did. Instead, I would sit and lie on each couch for several minutes. If the couch was going to reside in my house for several years it had to be comfortable. The fact that I was in a furniture store lying on couches with people around was of no concern to me. Neither was I concerned that other people around the store seeing a Rabbi lying on couches might be thinking some hidden camera reality TV show was being filmed in the store.

Each time Rachel picked a couch she liked I conducted the "couch test". I would sit for a while and then lie on the couch. When I found a couch that passed the test, Rachel would know since there would be a big smile on my face which I called the "smile of approval". If a couch received the "smile of approval" it meant that I could see myself lying on that couch for years to come. I thought that some of the sales people, having seen me conducting the test on a few couches, were placing bets on whether each couch I lied down on would pass the test.

After three stores, and many applications of the "couch test", we had narrowed the choices down to two. We went back to the store with the first of our two finalists and I again applied the couch test. Rachel then did her part by deciding which design and size she liked better. After another hour the decision was made. We had a winner. I thought some of the sales people might cheer and clap because they felt like they were part of our team, or they were just happy to finally get us out of their store.

As we got back into our car to drive home, the thought occurred to me that if new furniture was the price I paid for dealing with the Italian mob for Murray, should I end up with a more dangerous matter in the future, Rachel might announce that we are going car shopping. My side profession might start to get expensive.

When we got home, we decided to have a BBQ. I called my parents to invite them to join us. I started up the grill, got some chicken and hamburgers out of the freezer, cut up some vegetables and got to work. My parents arrived twenty minutes later. They both came out to the backyard to say hello. My mother then went inside to talk to Rachel. My father stayed outside with me by the grill.

"So Moshe, I hear Frank had a pre-wedding near melt down."

"How did you hear that Dad?"

"Moshe. Don't you know by now? I have ears everywhere. There are very few things that go on that I don't know about."

"You are like the KGB of rabbis."

"Are you working on any interesting matters in your non-Rabbi job?"

"I am helping Murray with a situation involving Italian mobsters from New York. Just what every Jewish mother hopes their child will grow up to do."

"That's what your mother always told me. She had little interest in you becoming a doctor or a lawyer."

"One of them is named Tony the Tilapia. How cool of a name is that?" I asked.

"Jews cannot have such names. Moshe the Mahi Mahi. It does not roll off the tongue as well."

"I agree."

"So what do these Italian gentlemen want with Murray?"

"They want to purchase large quantities of knishes from Murray at cost and want part of his profits."

"How did you respond?"

"I and my fellow Israeli mafia associates, who are Murray's silent business partners, indicated we are willing to consider a proposal."

"Oy vey. Let me guess. Eytan and some of his we are not really with the Mossad anymore, but maybe we are, but if we were we could not tell you and won't confirm or deny anything buddies dressed up as Israeli mobsters? I would have paid money to see this," said my father.

"I explained to Tony that this is our territory and they have to deal with us and our New York contingent."

"And how did they react?"

"Tony said he believed we could work something out."

"How nice of him. May I ask why they want to buy knishes from Murray?"

"The Balduccis are involved in the food business in New York. Steak and seafood. They claim to be interested in expanding into niche markets."

"For this alleged expansion they decided to pick kosher food from a deli in Miami Beach?" asked my father.

"That is what they told me. They seemed like genuinely honest individuals. Do you mean I have reason to doubt their sincerity?"

"Of course not. The bible teaches us to always trust what a mobster tells us. I believe that is the part right after King Solomon dealt with that whole baby issue."

"I must have missed that chapter in rabbinical school. I think I was playing hookie that day."

"Your mother always told you there was a price to pay for skipping school. Now you know she was correct. I hope you are happy with yourself."

I flipped the burgers and the chicken so they would cook evenly. I took great pride in my barbequing skills.

"I know it will come as a great surprise to you that I do not believe Tony," I said.

'I suspect even Tony does not believe Tony."

"I am trying to figure out what Tony and his pals are up to. So far I have no clue."

"Well, the prevailing view seems to be that the obvious answer Tony has presented is not the answer. By process of elimination one must then look to the not so obvious answer."

"Are you reading fortune cookies again in your spare time?" I asked.

"Confucius was part Jewish. Little known secret."

"I have an FBI agent Eytan connected me with and a sergeant in NYPD's organized crime unit looking into this as well."

"Do they have anything yet?"

"No, but they would both like to nail the Balduccis for something. It seems the Balduccis are quite good at keeping themselves out of trouble with the law."

"I am sure you will figure out what they are up to. After all, you are my son. Now let's eat."

I put the burgers and chicken on some plates.

My father and I carried the plates into the house to feed the masses. While we ate my mother asked how things were going with my private investigator work. I said fine, but did not get into any details regarding Murray's situation. It was bad enough to worry Rachel with the work I did. I certainly was not going to worry my Jewish mother as well. Worrying was an Olympic sport to my mother for which she had gold medals in numerous events including the 200 meter freestyle worry, the long jump worry, the backstroke worry and fencing while worrying. My mother was a diverse athlete. If my mother knew I was dealing with Italian mobsters, she would become the most decorated athlete in all of worrying history.

After dinner we all sat on our soon to be former living room furniture and watched the Dolphins game. Midway through the second quarter I decided I was going to miss my couch.

Chapter 18

Things had been relatively quiet with Todd Bronstein, as I had reported to his mother the prior week. However, from some chatter on the Facebook pages of a few of his troublesome friends, I got the sense they were planning something. It was time for me to talk to Todd.

I decided I would need some assistance from an electronics wiz Eytan knew by the name of Ephraim. Through some investigative digging I was able to get the cell phone number for one of Todd's troublesome friends. I gave the number to Eytan who passed it along to Ephraim. I gave Eytan the details of what I wanted Ephraim to do. Eytan said it would be no problem.

At 4:30 PM on Tuesday afternoon I drove up to a diner not far from Todd's school. I sat out front and waited in the car. At 4:45 PM Todd drove up to the diner, walked in and sat down at a booth. I waited a minute, walked into the diner and sat down in the booth across from Todd.

"Good afternoon Todd. My name is Rabbi Moshe Klein. Your friend Adam will not be joining you this afternoon even though you believe he asked you to meet him here to discuss an important matter."

"How do you know who I am and how could you know that Adam wanted me to meet him here?"

Just then the waitress came by the table to ask what we wanted. I told her I would have a cup of coffee. Todd did not order anything.

"I could tell you that I have magical Rabbi powers since I am one with the Lord, but you probably would not believe that. Let's just say I know certain people who have the ability to make it appear when you receive a text message that it came from a phone number in your contacts when in fact the text came from some other phone. Aside from being a Rabbi I am also a private investigator. As for how I know who you are, your mother hired me."

"Hired you to do what?" asked Todd.

"Your mother is concerned about you and the kids you have been hanging around with. She thinks you are going to get into trouble and ruin your chances of getting into an Ivy League school. Your mother would like me to keep an eye on you, find out what you are up to, and hopefully keep you out of trouble. Your principal would like the same. She is a very nice lady."

"My mom should stop worrying so much and find something better to do with her time."

"Well, being a parent I know that we worry. Being a Jewish parent, we worry even more. It's in our DNA. The crowd you are hanging around with does not give your mother reason to worry less. Wouldn't you agree?"

"Those guys just mess around. It's not anything serious."

"Nothing serious today could be very serious a week from now. Messing around usually does not go in the other direction towards innocent and free from trouble. It tends to escalate. So, here is the deal Todd. If you are determined to get into trouble, I, your mother and anyone else who cares about you can't stop you from doing so. We can't watch you twenty four hours a day. Here is my card. If you want to talk, give me a call. I am available any time."

I gave Todd my card, left a $20 bill on the table and got up from the booth. I told Todd that he could order something on me. I then walked out to my car, left the diner and drove to Best Buy to get a pay as you go cell phone. I decided it would be best if my dealings with Tony and his pals were conducted through an untraceable number should there be any problems.

Chapter 19

I decided to take Jacob to the Dolphins game that Sunday. I told Jacob he could invite one of his friends. Since I was getting the tickets I decided the same rule applied to me so I invited Eytan. We packed up the car that morning with the tailgate essentials and headed to the stadium. Since the Dolphins were playing the Falcons, the crowd was a bit lighter than would be there if we were playing the Jets or the Patriots, our arch rivals.

We found a good parking spot near a tree and got out the BBQ grill, some drinks and chips. Jacob and his friend threw a football back and forth while I cooked. Since I was wearing a yarmulke and looked like a Rabbi, a few of our fellow tailgaters asked if I was a Rabbi. When I said yes, they asked me to bless their barbeques in hopes of a good meal. Far be it from me to deny such a request, so I said a quick prayer asking that they should have a bountiful barbeque and not overcook their hot dogs.

I finished cooking and called over Jacob and his friend to eat. All four of us ate hot dogs and hamburgers. I wondered for a moment why we called them"hamburgers"when they are not made from ham. I thought that great mysteries such as this were on the minds of the founders of Google when they created their beloved search engine which with a few basic search terms and the click of a button could answer my hamburger naming question.

We finished our meal, packed up the BBQ grill and the chips, and walked to the stadium. Based on the looks I got from some people as we walked through the parking lot, it seemed they were thinking that the Dolphins needed help, and since nothing else had worked lately, perhaps the team was seeking some divine intervention and had hired a Rabbi to bless the team, the stadium, the field, the ball, the scoreboard, the referees and the coin for the coin toss, in hopes that something might work. I made a mental note to check on whether football teams had affiliations with religious figures in the community. If not, Rabbi Klein— the Rabbi for All Sports—might be my next endeavor.

After the first quarter, the Dolphins were down 7-0. On the bright side it could have been 21-0. We decided to take a break to get something to drink. We waited in line and got two sodas for Jacob and his friend. Eytan and I ordered two beers. I told the kids to go back to the seats since Eytan and I needed to talk for a minute. Eytan and I found a bench to sit on.

"I have been trying to figure out what the Balduccis are up to but I am drawing a blank. Do you have any ideas? Is there a disturbance in the Mossad force or some Mossad Jedi mind trick you can use on Tony to figure this one out?" I asked.

"Not that I know this since I can neither confirm nor deny my involvement with the Mossad at this present time, however, when I was involved which I can confirm, we were strictly prohibited from using Mossad Jedi mind tricks on Italian gangsters. That is in the policies and procedures manual, I believe on page forty-six."

"Who knew you were such a maven of rules?"

"I hold two merit badges from the Mossad for most accomplished follower of rules."

"I did not know the Mossad gave out merit badges," I said.

"They like to keep it quiet. The Mossad does not need a lawsuit from the Boy Scouts. We tried to get into the door to door cookie selling business, but the Girl Scouts are a vicious bunch when it comes to cookie sales. You don't mess with their bread and butter."

"I am shocked to hear that. I did not know the Mossad feared any group. Terrorists they will take on, but the Girl Scouts, no way. Back to the matter at hand. Do you have any thoughts on what the Balduccis are up to?"

"I do not. The obvious answer they gave us is not the answer. Thus, logic would dictate that we look for the non-obvious answer."

"You sound like my father since he told me the same thing. Do you two talk when I am not around?" I asked.

"Your father is a very wise man. Wise men do not need to talk to come to the same conclusion. Our wisdom and dashing good looks allow us to do such things."

"Your humility has always been one of your more impressive traits my friend."

"That is what your father tells me," said Eytan.

"I think we need to go back up to New York to do some surveillance on Tony and his organization so we can find out what they are up to."

"We would need to be stealth like for if Tony catches us he will not be pleased. Since I can confirm that I was with the Mossad at one point I know how to do such things."

"Do you think if I called the Mossad and told them how you torture me and everyone else you know by not confirming or denying that you are or are not still involved with the Mossad, that out of pity for those of us you torture they will just tell me if you are still involved?" I asked.

"Excellent question. I can neither confirm nor . . . "

"I should have known."

We went back to our seats and watched the rest of the game. The Dolphins lost 28-7. I decided to pray harder next game.

Chapter 20

Tuesday morning I stayed at the house to wait for the new couch to be delivered. Rachel had some errands to run. I sat on our soon to be old couch, relived memories of our good times together and enjoyed one final sitting before the new couch arrived. At 10 AM the delivery truck pulled up. The new couch was brought into the house. It looked like the couch we selected, which was a good sign. Since the old couch was being donated to charity, the two delivery men were nice enough to move the old couch out to the yard for me. Thirty minutes later the Salvation Army truck pulled up and our old couch was taken away. I was happy to know that while our couch would be missed, some lucky person or family would hopefully derive the same hours of pleasure from sitting on the couch as I did.

I got to my office around 11:30 AM. Lola had stopped off at the kosher bakery on her way to work and picked up some donuts. I grabbed a donut and contemplated my lunch options. Just as I was about to tell Lola to order from a local kosher deli, in burst Murray with a few brown bags in his hand. Murray had brought us lunch. I hoped that the cause of his trouble with the Balduccis, his beloved knishes, were among the food items he brought us.

Despite the usual near catastrophic banter between Murray and Lola, it seemed that Murray bringing lunch had a calming effect on Lola. Lola did not yell at Murray, call him names or threaten physical harm upon him. I made a mental note to advise Murray to bring food with him whenever he came to my office in order to keep Lola at bay. Murray gave two bags to Lola. He then walked into my office, gave me two bags and sat down.

"I thought I would bring you and Lola lunch. It is the least I can do for your helping me with the Balduccis."

"Murray, while not necessary, food from your deli is always appreciated. Speaking of which, are there knishes in one of these bags?" I asked.

"Of course," Murray said while smiling.

"Good. I am looking for answers to explain why

the Balduccis want in on your business and want large amounts of your knishes. No one has an explanation so I think I will go to the source."

I took out one of the knishes and unwrapped it. I turned the knish from side to side. I gave the knish a very serious look. I poked it and then held it up to the light. After looking at the knish for a minute, much to Murray's amusement, I put the knish down and said: "Knish. What do the Balduccis want with you and your family members? Tell me oh great knish. What secret power do you hold that Italian mobsters are so interested in?" I put my ear up to the knish but sadly it had no answers to my questions.

"Murray, it saddens me to report that this knish either has no information or has been sworn to secrecy. I shall have to solve this mystery the old fashioned way."

"And what is that? Murray asked.

"I shall confer with the Magic 8 Ball. It never steers me wrong. You shake it and you get the answers you seek."

Murray laughed. Lola who was busy eating her lunch also laughed.

"So what is the next step pending your consulting with the Magic 8 Ball?"asked Murray.

"Eytan and I will be going back to New York to do some surveillance on the Balduccis to see if we can figure out what they are up to."

"I can pack you some sandwiches and knishes for the trip."

"You are a good man Murray. Eytan will be delighted."

I kept eating and talked with Murray a bit more. When we finished talking, Murray thanked me again and left. Lola gave me a few messages for calls I missed which I returned. I then prepared for a class I was teaching the following night. Around 4:30 PM, Lola came into my office and told me that Todd Bronstein was here to see me. I told Lola to show him in.

"Good afternoon Todd. Have a seat."

Todd sat down in front of my desk and looked around my office.

"What can I do for you? Can I offer you a donut?"

The box was on my desk in case I got a mid-afternoon urge and did not feel like getting up from my desk to fulfill the urge. Todd took a donut, ate it, and sat silently for another minute. I knew he would talk when he was ready to and I was in no rush.

"My mom puts a lot of pressure on me with school and making sure I get into a good college."

"I am sure that she does. She wants the best for you."

"I know, but it gets to be a bit much sometimes."

"Have you tried talking with your mother to explain how you feel?"

"She won't listen to me. She is only focused on my getting into the right college."

"Your mother hired me to talk to you since she said you would not tell her what is going on. You think she won't listen to you, yet, both of you are talking to me. It seems the two people in this group who really need to talk are not doing so and have misconceptions about how the other one will react."

Todd thought for a minute about what I said.

"Do you have kids Rabbi?"

"I have two. A boy and a girl."

"Do you talk to them about what goes on with them?"

"I do. I think it is very important for parents to communicate with their children and for children to know that they can discuss anything with their parents."

"Have your kids ever gotten into trouble?"

"Everyone gets into trouble Todd. It depends on how you define trouble. Sometimes my kids don't do as they are told. If you are asking if they have ever gotten into serious trouble doing things that are illegal or wrong, the answer is no."

Todd thought for another moment.

"The kids at school are pressuring me to do things. They say it is just for fun and I should not worry. So far, it has not been anything that bad. I think they are looking to do worse things, like it is some sort of a challenge for them."

"You are a very lucky young man to have a family who loves you, wants the best for you and has the financial means to provide it. Sometimes kids in your position feel they need to rebel against that. You have started down that road. The question is whether you are going to continue on that path. You know where the path likely leads and it is not a good place. I am a former police officer Todd and I can tell you that the kids you are hanging around with will eventually want you do to something pretty foolish which will get you into big trouble, including trouble with the law."

Todd sat for a moment and thought. I waited since I

was in no rush and pushing him would not help.

"Rabbi, have you ever done anything illegal?"

"Well, years ago I bought a car. The salesman was a religious Catholic gentleman. Nice guy. I think he was so concerned that he would have to go to confession that week and tell the priest that he sold a car to a Rabbi and did not sell the car to me at a good price that I was able to negotiate an amazing deal. The price I paid was so good it should have been illegal since I was almost robbing the dealership. Does that count?" I asked.

Todd laughed. "Probably not," he said.

"Then the answer to your question would be no," I said.

"Thanks Rabbi."

Todd got out of the chair, walked out and closed the door behind him. I ate another donut and wondered what Todd was going to do.

Chapter 21

Wednesday evening I went to the gym with Eytan. We were doing the bench press. I could still bench a decent amount of weight, but Eytan was in a different league. Women would often look at him while we were at the gym. He did not seem to notice, or if he did, he played it off like he did not notice. I suspected Eytan did notice because he was very aware of his surroundings and did not miss much. I decided to ask him.

"Do you notice the women who stare at you when you work out or do you just ignore it for dramatic effect?" I asked.

"I accept the fact that women look at me. I am here to work out and I am focused on the task at hand."

"And ignoring their looks makes you intriguing?" I asked.

"I prefer mysterious, but intriguing works too."

"So you make the sacrifice to ignore these women

for their own benefit so they can create some intriguing mystery man fantasy in their heads?"

"When you put it like that it sounds so negative. I prefer to think of it as showing them my dedication to working out in the hope that they too will realize that they should focus on their workout. Thus, I am doing a community service by promoting good health."

"Your ability to rationalize things is astounding."

"I am a man of many talents."

We did a few more sets and then went to do some sparring in the room where aerobics and yoga are taught. Eytan was kind enough not to hit me too hard since whether he was still in the Mossad or not, if he hit me full force he would likely break something which would require me to seek medical attention. We sparred more for the cardio benefits than for real boxing purposes.

After a few rounds we sat down. I was breathing a bit heavy. Eytan looked like he had not just boxed a few rounds, but was walking around the mall shopping.

"When can you go to New York to do some investigating into the Balduccis?" I asked.

"My schedule is flexible for now, in between my community service to the female members of our gym."

"You are a saint. I can clear some things off of my calendar for next week. How about we fly up on Sunday and spend a few days?"

"Works for me. Maybe we can visit a gym in New York to see if my commitment to community service works up there as well, or if my talents are limited to the South Florida area."

"I suspect your talents travel across state lines," I said. "They might even work in other countries."

Chapter 22

Friday night we had some friends over for Shabbat dinner. Rachel cooked up a storm. She and Rebecca lit the candles. I did the kiddush and Jacob did the motzi blessing over the bread. We ate, discussed events of the week, the situation in Israel (a common topic of discussion), and sports.

After dinner we had dessert, sang the birkat hamazon and talked a bit more. After everyone left, I went out to the back yard to sit down and have some wine. Jacob came out after a few minutes to join me.

"Dad, can I talk to you about something?"

"Of course my son. I am always here to listen to you even though you have questionable taste in music."

"I bet your father said the same thing about you when you were a kid," said Jacob.

"Not true. We did not have music when I was growing up. We just had typewriters which we carried to school everyday up hill ten miles in the snow. Typewriters are not very musical."

"What is a typewriter?" asked Jacob.

"I am getting old. Anyway, what can I do for you my son?"

"Well, there is a girl in my class and I kind of, sort of . . ."

"You like her?"

"I do," said Jacob.

"Well then, she is a lucky girl."

"But I don't know how to tell her. I think she likes me. One of her friends told me that when we were texting."

"You know, back when I was growing up, when dinosaurs roamed the earth and we carried our typewriters around, we actually had to talk to girls either on the phone or face to face. We did not have texting and Facebook. I fear that your generation has lost the ability to talk to one another unless there is an electronic device involved."

"Did the dinosaurs try to take your typewriter?"

"You know, sarcasm comes from your mother's side of the family. You did not get this from me."

"Funny. Mom says the same thing about your side of the family."

"Alas, I think your mom may be right," I said.

"Mom says she is usually right."

"She is also right about that. Smart lady."

"Is that why you married her?"

"That and she had a really cool typewriter."

"So what do I do Dad?"

"Well, you could ask this young lady you like out on a date. Take her to a movie. Kids your age still go to the movies right? You don't just watch movies on your computers or on Netflix? If she is interested she will go with you. If she is not, she will say no or perhaps will give you some excuse to let you down easy. You could also get a group of your friends together to go to the movies and invite her if you want to see if she is interested in a non-date situation. Your other option is I post on the wall of her Facebook page that you like her."

"You wouldn't do that," said Jacob.

"Of course not. But the look of terror on your face for the brief second you thought about it was priceless."

Jacob laughed. We sat for a moment in silence.

"Thanks Dad. I will let you know how it goes."

"You're welcome. If you want to borrow my typewriter, let me know."

Jacob went back inside. I looked up at the sky and drank some wine. My boy was growing up. Soon he would be applying to college and heading out to find his way in the world. The world was a much simpler place back when we had typewriters.

Chapter 23

Sunday afternoon Eytan and I were on a plane back to New York. We packed all the necessary tools for doing surveillance on the Balduccis: cameras, binoculars, hats, fake noses and glasses to disguise ourselves. We also had sandwiches and knishes courtesy of Murray. We picked up our rental car, drove into the city, checked into our hotel and went to get some food. Since Jewish delis are as common in New York as mosquitos are in Miami, we had little trouble finding a place to eat.

I had called Sergeant O'Leary earlier in the week to get some information on where Tony and his gang spent their time so we could follow them around a bit. O'Leary gave me the addresses to the restaurants Tony and company frequented and some of the businesses he knew were paying part of their profits to Tony for "protection". Tony also had an office in the meat packing district out of which he ran the legitimate parts of the Balduccis's operations.

Eytan and I got up early Monday morning, went to the gym in the hotel, grabbed some breakfast and headed to Tony's office. We parked far enough down the block that we would not be noticed. Since Tony had seen us before, we had to do our best to stay out of sight. If we were spotted, and Tony thought Murray's Jewish mafia connection was spying on him, it likely would not bode well for Murray.

We waited for about an hour until two black Mercedes pulled up in front of Tony's office. Tony and Sammy got out of the back of the second car. Guido and another menacing looking individual got out of the back of the car in front. Guido and the other guy got behind Tony and followed him into the building.

Eytan and I had discussed whether we should try to get a tap on the phones in Tony's office. Eytan knew people in New York who had such skills, but we decided against it since the police and FBI probably had taps on Tony's phone, and Tony likely knew that so it was doubtful he or his associates were saying anything useful while on the phone. We also considered trying to hide a small microphone in Tony's office, but decided against that as well since any information we obtained from the mic, while possibly useful as to Murray's situation, could not be used against Tony in any court proceeding since it would be illegally obtained. Plus, if the mic was discovered, Tony might be even more careful which would make finding out what he wanted with Murray more difficult.

We also could not discount that Tony might be electronically savvy enough that he had his office regularly swept for bugs. That meant we had to do things the old fashioned way; knock on Tony's office door and ask if he would tell us what he wanted with Murray. Assuming Tony was not inclined to tell us, and did not try to shoot us, our only other option was to dig around until we found something useful.

We sat outside in the car for about two hours. Eytan walked down the street and got some coffee and bagels. Around 12 PM, Tony and his crew came out of the office, got into the cars and headed east. Based on the direction they were headed, we figured they were going to lunch at one of the restaurants O'Leary told us about. We pulled over half a block away from the restaurant so we would not be spotted. Even if Tony noticed our car, we figured he was probably used to police following him around so he would not think much of it.

When they finished lunch, Tony and his crew got back in their cars and headed to a few fish markets which we assumed the Balduccis had an interest in. Next, they stopped off at a small café to get some coffee. They sat outside drinking their coffee. We sat in the car drinking ours. Despite our differences, Tony and I agreed that coffee was a good thing. By 5 PM we had no information, had eaten some sandwiches and drank more coffee. So far, Tony had a rather boring day.

Tony and his crew then went back to the office for a bit, left at 7 PM and went to dinner at another restaurant. After dinner they went to a bar near their office and had a few drinks. By 10 PM, Eytan and I decided we had enough for one day and went to get something to eat. We got back to the hotel at 11:30 PM and both passed out soon after we got to the room.

The next morning we got up early, got some breakfast and headed to Tony's office. About thirty minutes later, Tony and his crew pulled up, got out of the cars and walked into the office. We sat and waited for an hour and a half before Tony came out. He and his crew drove to a small restaurant in the Village. About five minutes after they arrived, two cars pulled up and five gentlemen of similar appearance to Tony and his crew got out and headed into the restaurant.

"This place either gives a twenty percent discount on lunch to anyone who shows their mobster secret decoder ring or Tony is having a meeting with some people in his same line of work," I said.

"To be a fly on the wall while they discuss who is wearing the nicer suit."

"Should we go in, get a table and offer free Hebrew lessons to the winner of the nicest suit contest?" I asked.

"Let me give that some thought," Eytan said. "You are lucky it is not tax season or else you would have had to get one of your lawyer friends to protect you on this adventure."

"I might have been better off. If I get into trouble, all you can do is offer to do tax planning for the Balduccis and their ill gotten gains. A lawyer could at least sue them if they harm me."

"Perhaps, but the Balduccis probably have nicer suits than any of your lawyer friends."

After Tony finished lunch, we followed him around the city to a few other businesses, another café where he got his afternoon coffee, back to the office, and then to dinner. So far, we had not learned much except that

Tony was somewhat routine and rather boring for a mobster.

After dinner, Tony and his crew headed to a warehouse in the meat packing district not far from his office. They parked their car and headed inside. About ten minutes later another car pulled up. A man got out of the car, looked around to make sure no one was watching, and then opened the back door of his car. A large dog jumped out of the car. The man knocked on the door of the warehouse. After a minute the door opened a crack and the man and the dog were let in. Eytan and I had no clue what this was about, but it did look interesting. I suspected that Tony was not starting an adoption agency for stray animals.

I asked Eytan to write down the license tag of the car and told him it would be nice to know who the car belonged to. He dialed a number on his cell phone, told the person who answered that he needed to run a New York license plate and needed information on the owner of the car. He then hung up. A few minutes later Eytan's phone rang. He listened, thanked the person and hung up.

"The car belongs to Salvatore Mancini, a New York police officer. Officer Mancini is part of the K-9 unit.

He has been on the force for seven years."

"And what do you suppose Officer Mancini and his dog are doing with Tony and his crew?"I asked.

"Discussing details for the Balduccis's annual Passover seder and Italian wine jamboree?"

"Is jamboree a Yiddish term?"

"No, but it should be."

"Assuming you are wrong, we need to find out what they are up to. If, hypothetically speaking, we wanted to get into that warehouse after they leave, do you know anyone who could help us?"

"Rabbi, I am hurt. Are you suggesting that I may know someone who can pick a lock, disable an alarm, since we must assume there is an alarm, and take care of any other roadblocks there may be to our improperly gaining access to Tony's warehouse?"

"If you were still connected to the Mossad I would say definitely. However, since you can neither confirm nor deny such attachments, maybe your connections are not what they used to be."

"Are you trying to trick me into admitting some connection with the Mossad should I know someone who can get us into that building, for if I do not know anyone then I must not be connected with the Mossad?"

"I can neither confirm nor deny that I am doing such a thing," I said.

"You're lucky I like you."

Eytan dialed a number on his cell phone and told the person on the line that he needed to gain access to a warehouse which probably had an alarm and security cameras. Eytan said he would call the person back when the people left the warehouse.

"Seems I do have such connections. The person I called I know from my chess club."

"You play chess?" I asked.

"No. I just go there for the sandwiches. They also make good coffee."

Chapter 24

Eytan and I waited another hour until Officer Mancini and his four legged friend left the warehouse. A few minutes later, Tony and his crew left the warehouse. Eytan then called his friend to come meet us.

"Rabbi, we have been here two days and not once have I been able to put on my fake nose to fool Tony and his associates. This is very disappointing."

"But you have had the pleasure of my company for two days and quite a few New York bagels."

"I did have bagels. This is true."

"What? You don't like my company? I am shocked and hurt."

"I like your company. I just really like bagels."

Eytan's friend arrived ten minutes later. He got into the backseat of our car and introduced himself as Shimon. We decided to wait another few minutes to confirm that no one else was coming to the warehouse. When we were sure no one else was coming we got out of the car. Shimon was carrying a small duffel bag. We walked up to the door of the warehouse. Shimon inspected the lock. He went into his bag and took out some tools to pick the locks. Shimon had the door knob lock open within twenty seconds. The deadbolt took him forty-five seconds.

"I am assuming there is an alarm. I can disable it but I need to act fast before the signal goes to the alarm company and the police. We probably have thirty seconds to disable it once we open the door. Let me go in first," said Shimon.

Not knowing if there would be lights on in the warehouse, Shimon took out a flashlight and gave it to Eytan to hold to shine on the alarm code panel. Shimon took out a handheld device with a wire coming out from the bottom of the device with a small plug on the end of the wire. We counted to three and opened the door. The alarm started to beep. Shimon pulled open the panel and plugged his device into the alarm panel. The device ran numbers searching for the alarm code. After ten seconds it found the five digit code and set the alarm back onto safe mode.

"We're good. The alarm is deactivated," said Shimon.

"Nice work," I said.

"We are not done yet. We must also assume that your friends are concerned with the contents of this warehouse and have in place protective measures so that they know if anyone gets in. There is likely a surveillance system beyond this hallway. I need to tap into their computer system and take care of the cameras. I will need a few minutes."

Shimon took out a laptop computer, sat down on the floor and got to work.

"I located their wireless router," said Shimon. "Once I am connected to the router I can back my way into their server and deal with the cameras."

After another minute, and some furious typing on his keyboard, Shimon gave us an update.

"There are eight cameras. I am freezing the recording so that it will loop the image it now has. That will allow us to walk in without being picked up by the cameras. Once we are done I will reset the cameras so they won't know there was a break in the recording."

"Could you change their screen saver to say our suits are not made from real Italian material?" I asked.

"I could, but that might tip them off that someone was here," said Shimon.

"Fair point."

Shimon packed up his stuff. I said a quick prayer just to make sure that his computer magic worked and that we would not end up on tape for Tony's viewing displeasure.

We walked into the main part of the warehouse. Shimon gave me the flashlight and took out another one for himself. We walked around looking for clues, information or free suits in our sizes. There were boxes and crates everywhere on the first and second floors.

"We should probably open a crate or two to see what Tony is up to," I said. "Shimon, can your computer pop the top of one of these crates?"

"Eytan, you told me he was a Rabbi, but I did not know he was a comedian as well," said Shimon.

"Neither did I and I have known him for many years."

We walked over to one of the crates and popped it open. We shined our flashlights inside the crate and saw some shirts and blankets.

"I don't think Tony is shipping shirts and blankets to help those in need. I will bet you a $1 he is hiding something under there," I said.

We moved the shirts and blankets and found a large quantity of plastic bags containing white powder.

"Now it all makes sense. Tony is in the sugar business," said Eytan.

"We knew he was dealing drugs. The question is what Officer Mancini was doing here with them?" I asked.

We returned the contents of the crate and closed the top. I walked around a bit and found a garbage can near a table. There were a few small plastic bags on the table. Inside the trash can was some food that appeared to be fresh. There was some Spinach pie, what appeared to be a meat pie of some sort and another partial pie which smelled of onions.

"Are spinach pie, meat pie and onion pie typical Italian foods?" I asked.

"Let me consult my typical Italian foods guide," said Eytan. "It appears they are not."

"I think we have seen enough for one night. Let's wrap up here," I said.

We headed back to the hallway where we came in. Shimon took out his laptop and reset the cameras. He then plugged the device he used to shut off the alarm back into the alarm panel and turned the alarm back on. We quickly walked out the door. Shimon then took out the tools he used to pick the locks and locked the deadbolt.

"Like we were never even in there," said Shimon.

"That's why I call you," said Eytan.

"Happy to help. Rabbi, it was a pleasure meeting you."

"Thank you for your help," I said.

Shimon got in his car and drove off.

"He is a rather resourceful individual," I said.

"Shimon does have his talents."

"And where did he learn these talents?" I asked.

"Summer camp at the local JCC."

"You don't say? Funny, I did not see lock picking or computer hacking on the curriculum at our local JCC. I should tell them to add that to their program. The kids are missing out on useful skills they can take into the workplace."

We drove back to the hotel and went straight to bed. We woke up early the next morning, got some breakfast and headed to the airport. Our flight left at 10:30 AM. While on the plane I thought about whether Officer Mancini's visit to Tony's warehouse had anything to do with Tony's plan for Murray's knishes. I could not fit the two together but felt there might be a connection.

We landed around 1:00 PM. I dropped Eytan of at his house and thanked him for his help.

Chapter 25

After dropping Eytan off at his house, I decided to go into my office for a bit to see if there was anything important I missed while I was gone. Lola gave me my messages. Mrs. Bronstein had called for a status update. Frank called to thank me again for saving his marriage. He said the honeymoon was amazing. A fellow Rabbi from another temple called to discuss details for the mitzvah project a number of local temples were participating in on Sunday. We were fixing up a local women's shelter. I decided to call Mrs. Bronstein first.

"Hello Mrs. Bronstein. This is Rabbi Klein. How are you?"

"I'm well Rabbi. Tell me what you have found out about Todd."

"I spoke to his principal and did some checking on the kids he is hanging around with. Todd was supposed to meet one of his friends at a local diner last week. I magically appeared instead."

"And how did you do that?" Mrs. Bronstein asked.

"I am a Rabbi. I have my ways."

Mrs. Bronstein laughed a bit. It seemed my rabbinical charm was finally getting to her.

"I spoke with Todd about the choices he is making, gave him my card and told him to call me if he wanted to talk. He showed up at my office the next week. We had a good discussion. Todd feels that you put a lot of pressure on him to do well so he will get into a good school. I think he understands you want the best for him, but that is how he feels. He is rebelling by hanging around with the wrong crowd. Todd knows where the path he is on may lead. He has some choices to make."

"Well, I need you to stop him."

"Mrs. Bronstein, unless you are going to hire someone to watch Todd twenty four hours a day you can't stop him if he wants to do something that may get him into trouble. Todd has to take responsibility for his actions. He needs to decide whether he wants to go down that path. I am monitoring him and his friends to keep tabs on what they are up to. If I get information that Todd may do something he will regret, I will be there to encourage him to do otherwise."

"I just want what is best for him."

"I know you do. What matters now is what Todd wants for himself."

I told Mrs. Bronstein that I had an idea that may help. She agreed to pass along my request to Todd.

I wrapped up at the office and decided to call it a day. I wanted to go home to see my family. I pulled up to the house, walked in the front door and put down my bag.

"Where is the beautiful Mrs. of the house?" I asked.

"In the kitchen Moshe," said Rachel.

I walked into the kitchen, kissed Rachel and asked how she was doing. She was making dinner. I filled her in on the details of my trip to New York. I also told her about my conversation with Mrs. Bronstein. Rachel liked my idea for Todd. The kids arrived home about thirty minutes later. I hugged and kissed them and asked how they were doing.

We all had dinner and the kids filled me in on what was going on at school and other important details of their lives. We decided to rent a movie after dinner. I sat on the new couch with my family, waited for the movie to start and thought it was good to be home.

Chapter 26

Saturday morning services were moving along as usual. During the torah reading, I looked up and was delighted to see Todd and his mother walk into the shul and take a seat. Apparently Todd had agreed to my request which was a good thing since my sermon would be directed at him. We finished with the Torah reading and continued with the service. Thirty minutes later it was show time. I started my sermon by discussing the Torah portion for the week. I then reached the part directed at Todd.

"This week I thought I would discuss an important concept which we often overlook in our lives, responsibility. These days it is far too common that people do not take responsibility for their actions. We do not hold people accountable for what they do. We blame TV and video games for how children act. Why don't parents take responsibility for the TV shows their kids watch and the video games they play? The natural reaction these days is to blame others. It is always someone else's fault. It is not easy to look one's self in the mirror and say I am responsible for the things that I do.

The choices we make in our lives are ours to make and the consequences of our choices are ours to suffer. We cannot and should not blame others. By taking responsibility for our choices we will make better choices. We will treat the people in our lives better for if we choose not to treat them well it is our responsibility to deal with the consequences. If we choose a path that leads to trouble, we alone are responsible. Not our parents. Not our friends. Us and us alone. No matter what choices we make, we must take responsibility."

I finished the service and invited everyone to attend the kiddush we were having after the service courtesy of one of our members who was the sponsor. As I worked my way through the crowd, Todd and his mother approached me.

"Good morning Mrs. Bronstein and good morning Todd. I am so delighted that you decided to join us," I said.

"Thank you for inviting us Rabbi. This is a lovely temple," said Mrs. Bronstein.

"It is, however, I did not personally build it so I can only take limited credit."

"Rabbi, did your sermon have anything to do with me?"Todd asked.

"Responsibility for one's choices? The path we take we must be responsible for? I fail to see how that could have anything to do with you. Where do you get these ideas from Todd? Kids, Mrs. Bronstein. They think the world revolves around them and everything is about them. Such an attitude they have,"I said.

I smiled. Mrs. Bronstein and Todd did as well.

"Todd, I want to invite you to join us tomorrow for a wonderful event our temple and many others in the community are taking part in. We are renovating a local women's shelter. We will be painting, gardening and doing other work to give the place a nice new look. There will be lots of kids your age helping out."

Mrs. Bronstein looked at Todd.

"What do you say Todd? It sounds like a fun afternoon and a nice way to give back to the community."

Todd thought for a minute.

"I am deciding to attend Rabbi, and I take

responsibility for my decision. However, I take limited responsibility for the quality of any painting I will do since I have never painted before," said Todd.

"I think that is fair. I look forward to seeing you. Now, the two of you go get some food and mingle."

Chapter 28

On Monday I sat in my office with Tony's card in my hand. I decided it was time to call Tony regarding his offer to purchase knishes in bulk from Murray. I pondered leaving Tony a message that he should get a Costco membership and buy in bulk from them instead, but I did not suspect Tony had much of a sense of humor. I worked out what I wanted to say and then dialed the number. After a few rings my call went to voicemail. I was hoping for a message saying: "Hi, this is Tony the Tilapia. I can't come to the phone right now since I am out committing various criminal acts, but your call is important to me so leave a message and I will get back to you once my crime spree is finished." However, all I got was a beep.

"Tony, this is the Rabbi. Regarding our discussion some weeks ago when you visited South Florida, my people have a proposal. You may call me to discuss."

I then gave Tony the number of my pay as you go cell phone. About thirty minutes later my phone rang with a call from an unknown number. Since no one else had the number for my pay as you go cell phone, it was none other than Tony.

"This is the Rabbi," I said.

"Rabbi. This is Tony."

"I spoke to my people in New York. They will agree to your proposal but they want thirty percent which includes my cut."

"Thirty percent is rather steep Rabbi. I do not know that my people will agree to such terms," said Tony.

"Your people are welcome not to agree Tony. However, if they want to do business in our territory it will have to be on terms that are acceptable to us."

"Let me speak to my people. I will be in touch."

Tony then hung up the phone. I purposely told Tony that we wanted a high percentage because I knew he would come back with a counter offer. That would buy me more time to figure out what he was up to since I could then sit on his counter offer for a while.

I thought it was about time to check in with Agent Thompson. I called him and he said he could meet me for coffee at 4 PM. When I arrived, Agent Thompson had coffee waiting for me.

"Am I so predictable that you know I will want coffee every time we meet?" I asked.

"I checked their menu and they don't have knishes so I went with coffee."

"I will have you know that rabbis like apple pie as well. We even like milkshakes as long as we have them a certain amount of time after eating meat, although depending on who you ask the amount of time varies."

"Yours is a complicated people Rabbi."

"Not really. We just have a lot of rules."

"Seems you do. So have you learned anything about what Tony wants with your friend Murray?"

"Eytan and I did some surveillance in New York. We first learned that Tony has a pretty boring routine. The mob is not as exciting as portrayed in the movies. We also learned that Tony had a visit from a New York police officer who is a member of the K-9 unit. This officer brought his dog with him to visit Tony."

"Did the officer visit Tony in his squad car?" asked Agent Thompson.

"No. He was driving his own car. There was some food of the ethnic variety left over from their meeting."

"And how did you come to learn of the food?"

"Eytan knows people with many talents," I said.

"That he does. For the sake of wanting to nail the Balduccis I will not inquire of the specifics of how you gained such knowledge. It would not fall under my jurisdiction anyway. It would be an NYPD issue. The question is what an NYPD officer is doing with Tony? It would not surprise me that Tony has some police officers on his payroll, but why a K-9 officer?"

"Maybe it is not a K-9 officer per se, but this officer who is part of the K-9 unit travels with his fellow four legged officer for protection from people like Tony," I said.

"That could be. However, I would not discount that Tony is up to something."

"Agent Thompson, I am shocked. Do you mean to imply that Tony was not simply meeting this officer to make arrangements for a donation to the policeman's ball or to set up an endowment for the care and welfare of retired K-9 dogs?"

"Altruism is not one of Tony's better traits. Perhaps it is my years in government service that have made me a cynic."

"Perhaps, or keen instincts. I am not in government

service anymore and I share your doubts. I guess being a Rabbi makes one cynical as well when it comes to mobsters."

"Were there mobster type individuals in biblical times?" asked Agent Thompson.

"If there were, their suits did not cost nearly as much as Tony's."

"Have you told your contact at NYPD about the officer who visited Tony?"

"How do you know about my contact at NYPD?"

"Rabbi. I'm FBI. It's my job to know."

"No. I have not told him yet. I want the officer to keep doing whatever he is doing with Tony until I figure out what Tony is up to," I said.

"That's o.k. for now. However, I'm not sure how long you can keep that information away from NYPD. If an officer is rotten they need to know about it."

"I understand. Give me some time on this one. I think we can put it to use."

"Alright. We will give you some leeway for now. Do you want to give us the officer's name so we can keep tabs on him?" asked Agent Thompson.

"Not yet. I don't know how well trained he is and if he senses he is being watched or that he is under surveillance it may spook him and it may get back to Tony. Keep your distance for now."

"Will do. If you find out anything useful, let me know."

"I will."

Agent Thompson left a $5 bill for the coffee and headed out the door.

Chapter 29

Tuesday morning I got into the office early. I decided to run a background search on Officer Mancini. Nothing unusual came up. No criminal background, no connection to anyone with a criminal background. He was single. No kids. He lived in Brooklyn where he was born and raised. His parents still lived in Brooklyn. He had two brothers; one older and one younger. He did not own any real estate and did not have an expensive car registered in his name which meant that if he was on Tony's payroll, he was at least smart enough not to be buying flashy items that would be noticed as too expensive for someone on a cop's salary.

I called Mrs. Bronstein to see how Todd was doing. She told me the same story Todd did; that they had a nice chat and that Todd really enjoyed himself at the mitzvah project on Sunday. I suggested that she ask Todd if he would consider joining our USY group at the temple since it would be another way to keep him focused on staying out of trouble and would have him spending time with a less troublesome crowd. She said she would pass the idea along to Todd. I told her if she needed anything else she should call me.

I had lunch plans with my father. I met him at a kosher restaurant in Miami Beach which he liked to frequent. Kosher restaurants had become a more common sight in South Florida in the last ten years which made it easier to find a kosher meal aside from at one's house, or going to the one pizza place that everyone frequented. Since there is a growing Jewish population in South Florida that is increasingly younger, there is a need for such restaurants. Those who saw the opportunity had seized upon it and were doing well.

At 12 PM I left the office to meet my father. I parked, walked in and saw my father at a table towards the back. I said hello, sat down and looked at the menu. Our usual waitress Sarah came over to the table.

"Shalom. How are you today?" she asked.

"Good Sarah," I said. "And how are things with you?"

"Things are good. So Rabbi, what can I get you?"

My father and I both attempted to give our orders at the same time.

"You never get tired of doing that to me since you are both Rabbis. I should call your wives."

"Sarah," I said, "do you think my wife does not know I am like this? And where do you think I get it from? The guy sitting across the table who interrupted me giving you my order."

"He gets that from his mother," said my father. "I had nothing to do with it."

We then gave Sarah our orders one at a time.

"What's going on with Murray's potential unwanted business partners?" my father asked.

"Is that the politically correct way to refer to mobsters?"

"I believe so."

"Eytan and I were back in New York last week to do some surveillance on Tony and his gang. Tony had an off-duty NYPD officer from the K-9 unit pay him a visit."

"Do you think this officer is on the take?"

"Could be. I did a background search on him and he is not out buying expensive cars if Tony is paying him."

"What is the other option then?" asked my father.

"He is into the mob for money or is trying to pay off the debt of someone who owes the mob money," I said.

"Exactly."

"The question is which is it?" I asked.

"That is for you to find out my son. That is why you are the private investigator and I am just a humble Rabbi."

"If this officer is helping Tony to pay off someone's debt, why a K-9 officer?"

"Maybe Tony is looking for ways to get drugs shipped into or out of the port. Your officer may know someone who can help."

"Perhaps. I just have a sense that whatever Tony is up to is not that simple."

"Those are your rabbinical instincts which I instilled in you. Rabbinical instincts are sort of like Spiderman's spidey sense, just without the cool costume and ability to climb buildings."

"Tony wants to buy knishes from Murray. He claims the Balduccis are getting into the ethnic food business to branch out. In the warehouse where Tony met the officer, Eytan and I found left over spinach pie, meat pie and onion pie."

"So Tony invited the officer over for a meal. Dangerous but hospitable."

"You do look for the best in all people, don't you?" I asked.

"There is good in everyone, even those who do not seem to have any."

"So bringing food to feed a police officer who is violating the law to help Tony makes Tony a good person?"

"No. It makes him hungry and fond of pies."

"I think that meeting had something to do with the Balduccis's interest in Murray."

"Perhaps. So put on your investigator hat and go investigate my son. Your Rabbi hat may not be enough to solve this one."

Chapter 30

Since I needed to investigate, according to my father, I decided to go to the park and sit down for a bit to think. Quiet places like a park help the investigating process since they allow me to think and focus. I sat down on a bench. There were some kids playing in the park. A woman was playing catch with her dog.

What did ethnic foods, a police officer and a K-9 dog have in common? What use were those things to Tony? Tony was in the drug business. A K-9 dog would not tell Tony anything he did not already know since a K-9 dog would sniff out the drugs.

I kept thinking and looked at the woman with the dog. Since the dog had done a good job playing fetch, she called the dog over and give the dog a treat. The dog sniffed the treat and then took it from her hand and ate it. She then gave him another treat and the dog did the same routine.

As I watched I felt my rabbinical instincts, Spidey

investigator instincts or whatever my father called them, going off. I had an idea of what Tony might be up to. I needed to find a way to confirm my suspicions which would not be easy. I was tempted to walk up and thank the woman and her dog, but I was not sure whether the thank you was premature, and it would take too long to explain why I was thanking them so that she and her dog would understand.

I took out my cell phone and dialed Murray's deli. Murray asked if I had any news. I told him that I spoke to Tony and told Tony we wanted thirty percent of the profits he would make selling knishes. I told Murray my offer was designed to buy us time since Tony would come back with a counter offer. I also told Murray that I might have an idea of what Tony was up to and I would let him know if I confirmed my suspicions.

I hung up with Murray and dialed the Miami-Dade Police Department. I asked to speak to Sergeant Suarez. I knew Suarez from my time with the police department.

"This is Sergeant Suarez."

"Hi Jose. It's Rabbi Klein."

"Rabbi. Always good to hear from you. What can I do for you?"

"I am working on a case involving some mobsters up in New York who are trying to buy a particular food item in large quantities from a kosher deli located in Miami Beach."

"What does the mob want with food from a kosher deli?"

"That is the question Jose. I was wondering if you could help me try to figure it out."

"Sure. Tell me what you need."

"Do you happen to have some cocaine in the evidence room and a drug sniffing dog I can borrow for a few minutes?"

"Excuse me?" asked Jose.

"Let me explain," I said.

I told Jose about what I learned in New York while conducting surveillance on Tony. I then told him my theory of what Tony was up to.

"Rabbi, if you are correct that could pose a serious threat to efforts to stop drug trafficking not just in New York, but also in Miami if Tony's plan makes its way down here," said Jose.

"Yes it could. That's why I thought you would have an interest and might be willing to help me."

There was silence on the phone. I knew Jose was

contemplating the bureaucratic red tape he would encounter in helping me, so he was trying to find a way around it.

"Give me an hour and I will call you back."

"Thanks Jose."

I headed back to the office. I walked in and said hi to Lola. Once I got settled at my desk, Lola came into my office and sat down.

"I had the talk with Cindy."

"How did it go?"I asked.

"She reacted well. She is a good kid. I did as you suggested and told her that she can always talk to me and I will not judge her. I know you are right. All I can do is my best with her and hope it works out."

"If you would like, I can have Rachel's mother speak with Cindy as well. That woman has guilt powers that few people on this earth possess. When my mother-in-law is done with Cindy, she will remove the words 'sex' and 'drugs' from her vocabulary and may join the convent to become a nun."

"That would be nice. We don't have any nuns in my family,"said Lola.

Just then my cell phone rang. It was Jose.

"O.k. Rabbi. It took some work, but since you were

one of us I convinced the Chief that we need to help you with this one despite your unusual request. He too has great concerns for what might happen if you are right."

"Tell the Chief I appreciate it and he will be getting a nice present this Chanukah even though he is not Jewish."

"I will pass that along. Meet me at the station at 5 PM"

"Will do."

I hung up with Jose and called Murray. I told him what I needed for my experiment which he said he could get me. I had some other supplies I needed which I would pick up along the way. At 3:30 PM I left the office and headed to Murray's deli to pick up the items he said he would have for me. I then made a few more stops. I got to the police station at 4:50 PM and loaded the items for my experiment onto a cart. I then wheeled the cart into the station. The desk officer recognized me.

"Rabbi. To what do we owe the pleasure of a visit from you? And you brought gifts? Did Rachel cook for us?"

"You should be so lucky Tom. I am here to see Jose."

"Should I ask what is in the crate?"

"Jose is being kind enough to help me with an

experiment for a case I am working on. I am bringing in some supplies for the experiment."

"He is in his office. Go on back."

I went around the desk, down the hall and stopped in front of Jose's door which was open. I knocked and asked if anyone had ordered a Rabbi.

"Good to see you Moshe."

Jose picked up his phone and dialed a few numbers.

"Hi Mike. Do me a favor. Send Phil down to the evidence room with his dog. Thanks."

Jose lead the way down to the evidence room. We were let in by the evidence room clerk. Jose lead us to a table where I put down my stuff. The evidence clerk brought over some small bags with white powder.

"I had some drugs put into small bags like you asked Moshe."

"Good. Let me set up here and we will conduct our test."

I put the bags with the drugs into the crate which was filled with paper, packing material and other items, arranged the contents accordingly, and closed the crate. Phil entered the evidence room with his dog. Keeping his dog away from the crate, I told Phil what the test would involve. He said he understood. Phil walked his dog over to the crate. The dog sniffed for a minute and indicated to Phil that there were drugs in the crate. That was the easy and expected part. Phil then took his dog and walked out of the room.

I re-opened the crate, rearranged the drugs for my experiment, closed the crate and moved it to a different part of the room. I told Phil to come back into the room. He walked his dog up to the crate. The dog sniffed and did not indicate that there were drugs in the crate. Phil looked a bit confused.

"Are the drugs still in the crate?" asked Phil.

"Yes they are," I said.

"I don't understand. Rex has been on the force for years. He never gets fooled."

I opened the crate and showed Phil what I had done. My suspicion about what Tony was up to had proved to be correct.

"That is bad Sarge," said Phil. "Really bad. If the New York mob knows about this and if they can make it work, word will spread."

"It is has the potential to be a very big problem Phil. What are we going to do about this Moshe?"

"I don't know, but we need to do something."

Chapter 31

I went home after my experiment at the police station, walked into the house and said hello to Rachel and the kids. We all caught up during dinner. After dinner, the kids went up to their rooms to do their homework. Rachel and I went to the backyard to sit down and talk. I told her about my experiment which proved my suspicion about what Tony was really up to.

"What are you going to do Moshe? You need to tell NYPD about this so they can handle it," said Rachel.

"I don't think that is the solution. Without proof, all that NYPD would have is my experiment which would not be enough to get any state or federal prosecutor to charge Tony. Any lawyer with a decent law school education would have Tony out on bail and have the charges dropped soon thereafter."

"But you will tell them?"

"I will at the right time. I need to keep the Balduccis away from Murray. My knowing what they are up to does not guarantee Murray's safety and they will keep coming until they get what they want. If Murray does not voluntarily agree to help them, this will get much uglier."

"I know I don't need to say this, but I am going to anyway. You will be careful Moshe?"

"You know I will Rachel."

"Your family and your congregation need you. I don't know what we would do without you."

"Life would be far less entertaining," I said.

"That is true. Just promise me you will be careful."

"I will."

I kissed Rachel and held her hand. We sat for a while in silence. I was lucky to have a family who cared about me. I was not going to let the Balduccis do anything to change that.

Chapter 32

I got into the office early the next morning. I had been wrapped up with Murray's situation the last few days so I had catching up to do on my Rabbi related work. I had a meeting that afternoon with the principal of our day school to discuss our annual scholarship fund dinner. I also had to meet with the committee planning the Purim Festival. We had Jenny Cohen's bat mitzvah on Saturday so I had to meet with Jenny to review her Haftorah and her speech. Jenny's father ran a hedge fund. I was told that the party would be something to remember. It was turning out to be a busy Rabbi week for me.

My meeting with the principal went well. We discussed getting more sponsors for the dinner. The Purim festival committee meeting was another story. The co-chairs were arguing over whether to hire a musical act or a DJ, and if we did hire a musical act who it should be. They seemed to disagree about most details. The only thing I suspected they did agree on was that there should be hamentashen at the festival, although they probably disagreed on what flavor. I considered putting the co-chairs in time out to let them cool off for a bit, but time out does not work well on adults since they can just get up and walk out of the room. It is even less effective on volunteers for an event. After I questioned the reasons for their opinions of what we should do for the festival, each co-chair begrudgingly saw that they needed to work together to come up with the best solution for the event, even if that meant not getting their way.

With all the committees we have I wondered if we should set up a committee whose sole function would be to oversee all of the other committees. We could call it the Committee of All Committees or the Super Duper Committee.

Thankfully, practicing with Jenny for her bat mitzvah was far more peaceful than the Purim festival committee meeting. Jenny did a good job with her haftorah and I knew she was ready. We went over her speech and then I told her I would see her Saturday morning. Jacob had a basketball game that night so I had to head out in case traffic was backed up, which was usually the case at rush hour in South Florida.

I got to the game just in time for tip off. Jacob was starting. He looked good. Practice over the last few months had paid off. He was handling the ball well. Watching him made me think of my football career. Sometimes I missed playing since my football career had not worked out like I hoped having blown out my knee before I made it to the NFL. Over the years I had wondered how different things would have been if I had played pro football. Would I have become a Rabbi after my NFL career finished? I did not know any former NFL players who were rabbis so I may have been a novelty. Being a Rabbi with a Super Bowl ring would have been pretty cool.

At the end of the first half, Jacob's team was up by 10 points. His team won by 14 points. When he came off the court I gave him a high five and told him he played well. He asked if we could go get pizza to celebrate. Far be it from me to say no to the highest scoring member of the team that night, so I said yes.

We walked into the restaurant and were greeted by the owner who I had known for many years. We were shown to a table and I said hello to a few people I knew who were also having pizza. Jacob and I sat down and looked at our menus. We ordered a large pizza with mushrooms and onions. Luckily Jacob and I had similar taste in pizza toppings. I believe a pizza with some toppings on one half and other toppings on the other half ruins the symmetry of a pizza since it interferes with the yin and yang of the pizza.

Jacob gave me a recap of the game. He said that he was shooting better during the last few months which I told him I agreed with. He then told me if they won two more games they would be in the playoffs. I suspected they had a good chance of getting into the playoffs.

"So Dad, I took your advice," said Jacob.

"You voluntarily cleaned up your room so you mother does not have to tell you to do it for the thousandth time?"

"No. I asked the girl I told you about to a movie."

This was far bigger news than if Jacob had actually volunteered to clean his room.

"And what happened?" I asked.

"She said yes."

"Congratulations. Seems your Dad does know something after all."

"Seems you do."

A moment later our pizza came out. Jacob took the first slice as was our usual system. I then took a slice, took a bite, chewed and looked at Jacob eating his pizza. My son was growing up. He was going on his first date. I was not sure I was ready for it, but I knew I did not have a choice but to accept it.

We finished up our pizza and headed home.

Chapter 33

I met Eytan at the gym early the next morning. We did our workout with the weights and then went to punch the bag. I filled him in on my experiment at the police station.

"Jose let you do all that?"

"He did," I said.

"You former cops get such special treatment. Seized drugs and your own K-9 dog to play with."

"They even let me turn on the siren in the squad car."

"This is what my tax dollars are paying for. How nice."

"I can have Phil bring his K-9 friend over to your house to play. Would that make you feel better?" I asked.

"You are too kind. So you think you figured out what Tony is up to?"

"I do. If I am right, it could cause major problems

for the authorities trying to stop drugs from being shipped into and moving around the country."

"Have you heard from Tony?" asked Eytan.

"He has not responded to my offer of thirty percent of his profits."

"Maybe he is preparing a PowerPoint presentation with colorful charts showing why thirty percent is an unreasonable amount. You have to pick the right colors, make the text appear from different directions. A good PowerPoint presentation takes time."

We finished our workout, got changed and left the gym. I headed to the office. Around 10:30 AM my pay as you go cell phone, or as I liked to call it, the "Tony hotline", rang. I thought Tony might be calling to get my e-mail address so he could send me his PowerPoint presentation. I took a moment to get into my Israeli mobster mind set, and then answered the call.

"This is the Rabbi."

"Rabbi, it's Tony. I spoke to my people about your offer and they cannot accept it. The best we can do is fifteen percent which is a very generous offer. You are getting a piece of the action for no work."

"My people will not accept an offer that does not have a two in front of it. If you want to be involved in our business and in our territory, this is the way it has to be."

"Rabbi, I am sorry to hear that. I can tell you that my people will not go higher than fifteen percent. I really think you should reconsider. If we cannot come to terms, it would be most unfortunate."

"Unfortunate for who? You're not threatening me Tony, are you? That would be unwise."

"No, of course not Rabbi. Let's just say that it would be unfortunate for your pal Murray."

"Tony, you are putting your operation at great risk if you do anything to Murray. I suggest you go back to your people and tell them to raise their number."

"I will do so Rabbi, but for Murray's sake I think your people better rethink their number. We will be in touch."

Tony hung up. Mobsters had no manners. He did not even say goodbye.

I called Murray and told him we needed to talk. I said I would stop by the deli for lunch. I left the office at 12 PM and headed to the deli. I walked in and was seated in a booth. Murray came over after a few minutes.

"Hi Rabbi. Any news from Tony?" Murray asked.

"Yes. Tony made a counter offer of fifteen percent which I told him was insufficient."

"How did he react?"

"Not well."

"Did you figure out what he is up to?"

"I think so."

"So what is it?"

"I would rather not say in case you get asked. The less you know the better that way if you say you don't know anything you will appear truthful."

"Do I have something to be worried about Rabbi?"

"Tony did not like my rejecting his counter offer. I told him his number needs to have a two in front of it. He then said it would be unfortunate for you if we did not work out a deal."

"If a mobster is using the word unfortunate and my name in the same sentence I think I have a lot to be worried about," said Murray.

"I think I have one more round of negotiations with Tony. We can't tell him you will do business with him because he will immediately come down here wanting to buy large quantities of knishes and you can't be doing business with the mob. The various authorities who are looking to nail Tony would not look kindly on that and you may end up with criminal charges being brought against you."

"Criminal charges may be a more favorable option to being killed by Tony and his fish named friends. With a good lawyer I will at least have a shot in court."

"I understand your concern Murray, but we need to find a way to take Tony down. If we don't, he will keep coming after you and wanting in on your business."

"I know Rabbi, but I'm scared. I am a simple deli owner. I don't know how to deal with the mob. Now I have to look over my shoulder everywhere I go."

"Harming you does not do Tony any good because that means he cannot get knishes from you. Tony needs you around Murray, whether he wants to admit it or not."

"I guess, but I am still very worried."

"I know. Let's see what Tony comes back with."

"O.k. I am going to get back to the kitchen. Lunch is on me. Enjoy."

"Thanks Murray."

I ate my lunch and decided it was best not to tell Murray that I was also worried. I could not watch Murray twenty four hours a day and the police would not watch him because there was no direct threat.

However, Murray needed some type of protection.

I finished my lunch, thanked Murray, and headed back to the office. Along the way I called Eytan and asked if he would inquire if his pretend Israeli mob friends, along with myself and Eytan, could work in teams of two over the next number of days to watch the deli as Murray closed up so we could make sure that he got home safely. Eytan said he would make some calls and would get back to me.

I headed back to the office. I had to work on the torah portion for the week and my sermon for Jenny Cohen's bat mitzvah. Eytan called at 3 PM to tell me that we were set up for Murray's protection detail. He and I would take one shift and his four associates would split the other two shifts. I called Murray and told him that we would be keeping an eye on him for the next few days. He sounded relieved.

Chapter 34

The first few days of Murray's protection detail went without incident. Tony had not called me back so I was unsure if he was planning to make a move on Murray, or was speaking to his accountant to determine if paying the Israeli mob would have too much of an impact on his bottom line.

On the fourth day of our protection detail, I called Murray as Eytan and I were on our way over to the deli.

"Hi Murray. We are on our way."

"O.k. I am just cleaning up. We are open for another thirty minutes."

"We will see you in a bit."

Just as I finished my sentence I heard Murray say something that made the hair on the back of my neck stand up.

"Oh no. Tony is here," said Murray.

Murray kept the phone to his ear so I could hear his

conversation. I pushed the pedal to the floor to get to the deli as quickly as possible.

"Hi Tony. What can I do for you? . . . What? . . . I'm sure we can work it out . . . My business partners are not unreasonable."

Then, I heard Tony.

"Let's go Murray. We are going to take a little ride."

The phone then dropped and Murray was gone. Since I took the call on the Bluetooth in my car, Eytan also heard the call. He did not look pleased. We got to the deli ten minutes after Murray dropped the phone. We ran into the deli and found one of the cooks who we knew in the kitchen.

"Hi Sam. Did you hear anything?"

"Hear what? I was in the back cleaning up. Where is Murray?" asked Sam.

"Sam, Murray is going to be gone for a bit. Call Sheila and tell her she in charge until she hears otherwise."

I could tell by the look on Sam's face that he knew something was wrong, but he was not sure if he should ask.

"Is Murray going to be o.k. Rabbi?"

"We will do our best to get him back. Sam, I need you to promise me that you won't call the police. They cannot help Murray. We need to take care of this. Can you promise me that?" I asked.

"Of course Rabbi. I know Murray trusts you. Bring him back safely."

I turned to my left and saw the phone Murray dropped which was off the hook. I walked over and hung up the phone. I looked over at Eytan. He had a look on his face that I suspected he got when he was on missions for the Mossad. If this was Eytan's "game face", it was a very scary face. Tony had no idea what he just done. He took the owner of the favorite deli of a former or possibly current Mossad agent, and that agent had other current or former Mossad agent friends who would do as he asked to get Murray back. I was not sure if I felt more concerned for Murray's or Tony's safety.

I told Sam to lock up. Eytan and I then headed to the car.

"We need a plan," I said.

"Tony will call with a demand. Until we know what he wants and where Murray is we can't make a move. While we wait we can put our plan together."

I knew Eytan was right, however, what bothered me was that until Tony called we did not know what we were planning for. I decided it was time to call Agent Thompson.

"Agent Thompson. It's Rabbi Klein. I am sorry for the late call. Tony took Murray."

"When?"

"About twenty minutes ago. We thought Tony might try something so we were escorting Murray home each night from the deli. If I had to guess, Tony might have been watching and saw our protection detail and got there early tonight to grab Murray before we arrived."

"Have you got a plan?" asked Agent Thompson.

"We are working on it. We need your help."

"Coffee in thirty minutes?"

"See you there."

Eytan and I drove to the restaurant and got a booth. Agent Thompson arrived a few minutes later.

"Eytan. Good to see you, although I wish it was under more pleasant circumstances," said Agent Thompson.

Eytan nodded.

"Rabbi, why don't you fill me in on what has been going on with you and Tony."

I told Agent Thompson about my thirty percent offer to Tony and his counter offer of fifteen percent. I also told him that I thought I had figured out why Tony wanted to buy knishes from Murray.

"Interesting theory. Do you have anything to back it up?"

"I do. I conducted a test at Miami PD which seemed to prove my theory. They are quite worried I may be right."

"As am I. Particularly in a city like Miami where the drug trade from Latin America is enormous. So what's your plan to get Murray back?"

"We don't know yet. We have to wait for Tony to call and make his demand. We assume he will want a meeting in person," I said.

"I think he will. That will be a rather dangerous meeting for you to attend. However, Tony has no idea who he has upset. With Eytan as part of your team, I am not sure if I am more worried for the safety of Murray or Tony."

"Seems you and I agree on that point."

"We need to take the Balduccis down," I said. "They won't stop unless they get what they want from Murray. If I am right about what Tony is up to, they are doing this to other people as well. He needs to be stopped."

"Tony presumably kidnapped Murray and is likely taking him across state lines. That is a good start. If you can get us something that proves your theory of what Tony wants with Murray's knishes, it should be enough to put him and his pals away for a long time and will help us bust up the Balduccis."

"You think Tony is taking Murray to New York?" I asked.

"Tony will not play in your ballpark. He likes home field advantage. He can move Murray around much easier in New York. He knows the territory. My guess is your meeting will be in New York."

"I will get in touch with my contact in NYPD's organized crime unit."

"That is probably a good idea. I can put my resources on this to take Tony down, but local police in New York will have their ear to the ground better than we will. Under normal circumstances, I would tell you that local police or the FBI should be taking this over. However, you and Eytan can work quicker than we can to find Murray. I also know Eytan will bring some of his friends to help. Eytan, I won't get in your way on this one."

Eytan nodded.

"As soon as you hear something, let me know. I can

have resources available in New York if you are going to make a move."

Agent Thompson took another sip of his coffee, got up, and walked out of the diner. I paid the bill and Eytan and I went back to my car. I called Rachel to tell her that I would be home in a bit. I then called Murray's wife.

"Deborah. It's Rabbi Klein."

"Rabbi, where is my Murray? He should have been home an hour ago. Is he o.k.?"

"Tony took him from the deli."

Murray told Deborah about the situation with Tony since if anything happened he wanted her to be able to contact me.

"Oh no. My Murray. What's going to happen to him Rabbi? You have to get him back for me." Deborah started to cry.

"Our guess is Tony is taking Murray to New York. Eytan is with me. Tony will call us to tell us what he wants for us to get Murray back. We just met with an FBI agent who I have been in contact with since the situation with Tony first started. I also have someone in the organized crime unit at NYPD. We will be calling him as well."

"Eytan, tell me you will get my Murray back alive.

Murray told me how much you love eating at the deli."

"Deborah, we will get him back," Eytan said.

Eytan's statement had a calming effect on Deborah.

"I am not sure if I am more worried for the safety of Murray or Tony," said Deborah.

For the first time all night I smiled. Tony had no idea what he was in for.

"We will be in touch Deborah."

Chapter 35

Murray was in a car with Tony, Sammy and Guido with a bag over his head. He could not see where they were going. No one was talking. They had been driving for about twenty five minutes, which meant that they were either in the southern part of Miami or somewhere near Fort Lauderdale. A minute later the car stopped. Guido pulled Murray out of the back seat and told him to walk. Murray's hands were handcuffed. He walked with Guido leading him since the bag was still over his head. After a few seconds Guido told Murray to stop and he pushed Murray down into a chair. The bag was pulled off of Murray's head. Tony was standing in front of him with Sammy at his side.

"Murray. So nice of you to join us this evening," said Tony. "I apologize I did not call ahead to make a reservation to take you away from the deli. Excuse my bad manners."

Murray sat in the chair looking at Tony. He was not sure where this was going, but he did not think it was good.

"Murray, here's the deal. Your Israeli business partners made me an offer of thirty percent of the profits I will make from knishes I buy from you. That was an unacceptable offer. I countered at fifteen percent. Mine was a very generous offer, yet, the Rabbi did not accept. So, I needed to send the Rabbi a little message. It's just business. You understand, don't you Murray?"

Murray nodded.

"So tell me Murray, how did you get involved with the Israeli mob?"

"I wanted to expand the deli some years ago. A friend told me about someone he knew who could arrange financing. Also, this person would make sure that no other deli opened up in my area. In return, they would get a piece of the profits from the deli."

At that moment Murray was quite thankful that he and the Rabbi had worked out a cover story should this issue come up.

"Murray, I am surprised. You seem like such a nice mild mannered, law abiding citizen. Yet, you are in business with the mob. Looks can be deceiving. However, know this Murray. I get what I want. If someone messes with that, people get hurt. About that I am deadly serious."

Tony hung on the word "deadly" long enough to emphasize the point.

"You are now going to take a little trip Murray."

Guido stuck a needle into Murray's neck.

"Ow," said Murray. "What did he stick me with?"

"I can't have you making noise during this trip so you are going to take a nap. Sweet dreams Murray."

Murray began to lose focus and then the room went black.

"Load him up boys," said Tony.

Guido and Sammy took Murray out of the chair, taped his mouth and tied his legs together. Then, they put Murray into a crate. They nailed the crate shut and put the crate on a lift. A moment later there was a knock on the door. Guido opened the warehouse bay door and a cargo truck backed into the warehouse. The driver got out and opened the back of the truck. Sammy drove the lift over to the truck and loaded the crate into the truck. The driver, Guido and Sammy then moved the crate to the side and the driver pulled a belt around the crate to secure it so it would not move during the drive.

The driver got into the truck, pulled out of the warehouse and headed to Miami International Airport.

Chapter 36

I got home around 12:30 AM. Rachel was waiting for me in the living room, sitting on our new couch.

"What happened Moshe?" she asked.

"Tony took Murray. He grabbed him before Eytan and I got to the deli. I think Tony was watching the deli and knew when we would be there."

"Have you spoken to Deborah?"

"I have. I told her we will get Murray back."

"Do you think Tony will kill Murray?"

"No. Tony wants to buy knishes from Murray. This is how Tony negotiates. Tony wants me to know that if I don't voluntarily give him what he wants, he will get it one way or the other."

"I'm scared for Murray, but I am also scared for you. This is the mob we are talking about. This is a very dangerous situation you are in."

"I know, but I have Eytan and his associates on my side. Between Tony and Eytan, I will put my money on Eytan any day of the week."

"I agree, but I am still worried."

"I have to get Murray back Rachel. I also need to take the Balduccis down. They won't stop at this. They will always want more."

"That's the former police officer side of you talking. That's not your job Moshe. Let the authorities do it."

"They have tried Rachel. They can't get anything on Tony that will stick. If I am right about what Tony wants with Murray, this will put him away. I will be careful. The FBI is in if we have something and I believe NYPD will be there as well."

"This family needs you Moshe. If anything happens to you I will kill you myself."

"Good to know. I will advise Tony of that. Perhaps that will change his mind about things."

"I'm a Jewish mother and the wife of a wonderful caring man. Tony has no idea who he is messing with."

Chapter 37

I arrived at my office the next morning and said hi to Lola. She could tell something was wrong.

"Rabbi. Are you o.k.?" she asked.

"Tony took Murray last night. We think he is on his way to New York."

"Oh no. What are you going to do?"

"Tony will call and will likely want a meeting. Until then, we have to wait."

"I know Murray annoys me sometimes, but I hope he will be o.k. You will get him back. I know you will."

I went to sit at my desk to think. I was not sure what to think about but knew I should be thinking. What was Tony going to do? I did not think he would kill Murray. Murray was a bargaining chip. In the end, Tony wanted the knishes and he needed Murray alive to get them. Tony wanted me to know that he was in charge. This was a control play pure and simple. Assuming Tony was going to set up a meeting with me, he was going to do his best to convince me that we either give him what he wants, which may be at a number lower than the fifteen percent he previously offered, or else bad things would happen.

A few minutes later the Tony hotline rang.

"Rabbi, it's Tony. I am not a patient man. When you did not come back with another offer, I decided I needed to send you a message to let you know how serious I am. I now have something you want."

"Where is Murray?"

"He is safe, for now."

"I am sure it will come as no surprise that my people are not very happy with your actions Tony. We want Murray back."

"I am sure you do. Seems we each want something. I think we need to meet to discuss the issue."

"Where and when Tony?"

"I will be in touch."

Tony hung up. I was relieved, although not surprised to know that Murray was alive. I called Eytan and told him that Tony had made contact and that he would be in touch with meeting details. I then called Deborah to let her know that Murray was alive. She was relieved as well.

About two hours later the Tony hot line rang again.

"We will meet in two days in New York at 8 PM. Just you. None of the other biblical characters you hang around with," said Tony.

"You expect me to come meet you without my associates? What kind of fool do you take me for Tony? Let me ask you a question. Would you attend such a meeting by yourself?"

"Of course not. But you aren't holding someone I hope will be returned to me alive and in one piece."

Tony then gave me the address of the meeting and hung up. I called Eytan.

"The meeting is in two days in New York."

I told Eytan the address of the meeting location.

"This will be fun," said Eytan.

Chapter 38

That night, Eytan and I met with the other members of our Israeli mob to plan our take down of the Balduccis and how we would get Murray back alive. The location for the meeting with Tony was the warehouse where Eytan and I saw Tony meet with Officer Mancini. Since we knew the set up, we planned to use that to our advantage. We drew the inside of the warehouse to work out the details. After an hour we had a plan.

Since Eytan and his friends could not bring guns on a commercial flight, Eytan had to make arrangements for us to get supplies in New York. He called Shimon and told him what we needed. Eytan also told Shimon we would need some additional help from him to make our plan work. Shimon said he was happy to help.

We booked a flight to New York for the following day. I called Agent Thompson to tell him where and when the meeting with Tony would be held. I then told him our plan. He said he would get in touch with the FBI office in New York to make arrangements.

I got home late that night. I looked into Rebecca's and Jacob's rooms. They were sleeping. I stood in front of each of their rooms for a moment. Not that I expected anything to go wrong in New York, but I felt compelled to look in on them. They did not know the details of what had happened to Murray and I felt it best that they not know. Their mother would do enough worrying.

I walked into the bedroom and quietly got into bed. Rachel stirred.

"You're back," Rachel said.

"I am."

"Any update?"

"The meting with Tony is in two days in New York. Eytan and I and the rest of his team fly up tomorrow. The FBI has been notified. I will speak with NYPD in the morning. We are ready to go."

"You will be careful, won't you?"

"You know I will. I plan to be back here with you and the kids for a nice Shabbat dinner on Friday."

"Good."

Rachel smiled, kissed me and went back to sleep. I went over the plan in my head a few times to see if there were any holes. I was dealing with five former or current Mossad agents so if they approved the plan I felt comfortable it would work. Eventually I drifted off to sleep.

I woke up the next morning and told the kids that I would be going to New York for business and would be back in a few days. Not knowing what was going on, they did not think anything of it, wished me a good trip, and finished getting ready for school. Rachel dropped them off and then came back to say goodbye to me. I told her I would be careful, that I loved her and then kissed her goodbye.

I picked up Eytan and we headed to the airport. Along the way I called Sergeant O'Leary to catch him up on what had happened and to ask for his assistance.

"Well Rabbi, it seems you have been rather busy. If you think you can take down Tony, we are in."

"I will call you when we get to New York to work out the details."

Eytan and I got to the airport and parked. We went to the gate and met the other members of our team.

We went through security, waited at the gate and boarded the flight. Once we were in the air it occurred to me that if there was a terrorist on our plane, he or she would really have picked the wrong flight to be on with five former or current Mossad agents on board. That is one terrorist plot that would go horribly wrong.

Chapter 39

We landed at 12 PM and headed to Shimon's office in Brooklyn. As promised, Shimon got the supplies we would need. Eytan and I had a meeting later that afternoon. Shimon and the rest of the team would get the supplies ready and work out the details for our meeting with Tony. Eytan and I would come back to Shimon's office when we were done with our meeting.

Eytan and I got some food. We then drove to a house in Brooklyn and waited. About an hour later Office Mancini showed up with his dog. As he got out of his car, Eytan and I got out and walked up to him.

"Officer," I said.

"Yes?"

"My name is Moshe Klein. I am a private investigator from Miami. We need to talk."

"About what?" asked Officer Mancini.

"We know about you and the Balduccis."

"What are you talking about?"

"Officer, I am a former cop. Let's not play games. We can do this the easy way or the hard way. The easy way involves you helping us. The hard way means we go to NYPD and the FBI and let them have at you. If you come clean you can work a deal. If you don't, Tony will throw you under the bus to get a better deal for himself."

Eytan showed Officer Mancini a few of the photos we took of him while he was visiting Tony. I could tell by the look on his face that he knew he was in trouble.

"O.k. Come in."

We walked into Officer Mancini's house. He showed us to the kitchen table. We sat down. I told Officer Mancini my theory of what Tony was up to and why he wanted Officer Mancini's help. Officer Mancini nodded his head indicating that my theory was correct.

"My father owes the Balduccis money. I knew nothing about it. My father fell behind in getting them the money. One day I get a visit from Tony who tells me I have two choices. One, I let him use my dog for something he is doing, or two, he will kill my father. I had no choice."

"We understand," I said. "I have someone I need you to talk to."

I took out my cell phone and dialed Agent Thompson.

"Hi. It's Rabbi Klein. I am sitting in New York with someone you need to talk to."

I handed the phone to Officer Mancini.

"Officer, this is Agent Thompson with the FBI. He can help you."

Officer Mancini took the phone and told Agent Thompson what he knew about Tony's plan. Officer Mancini handed the phone back to me.

"Rabbi, stay there with the Officer. I am calling the Manhattan field office. They will have some agents come out to pick him up. We will take him into protective custody."

About forty five minutes later there was a knock on the door. Two men in dark black suits showed their badges. They asked Officer Mancini to come with them. They put him in the back of the car and drove off. Eytan and I got back in our car and headed to Shimon's office.

When we walked into Shimon's office, guns were spread out on the table. There were also multiple knives and other assorted gear. I assumed all the gear had been checked and cleaned by Eytan's associates. The plan was for us to take a ride at 11 PM to the location of the meeting so that we could figure out where everyone would be while I met with Tony. As I said to Tony, only an idiot would show up alone to a meeting with him, and my mother did not raise an idiot Rabbi for a son. Tony did not need to know that I was not alone. As long as he thought I was, he would not be expecting the unexpected.

At 11 PM we got ready to head out. Everyone took a gun just in case we ran into trouble. We got in two cars and headed to the meeting location. We arrived at 11:30 PM. We pulled up a block away, parked the cars and waited. We agreed to wait fifteen minutes to make sure that no one was in the area and that no one came out of the warehouse. When things looked clear, Eytan, Shimon and I got out of our car. The other members of our team knew to wait in their car until we gave them the all clear signal.

Shimon carried a bag with him I had labeled his "bag of tricks". The first thing out of his bag was a device I did not recognize.

"What is that Shimon?" I asked.

"Thermal scanner. This will tell us if there is anyone

in the building. It scans for heat and will pick up body temperature if anyone is in there. I thought it best we know before going in and surprising someone."

This part of the plan had apparently been worked out while Eytan and I were meeting with Officer Mancini. It seemed the other members of our team had put their time to good use. Shimon turned on the scanner and moved closer to the building to see if he picked up a reading of anyone in the building. After a minute he turned off the scanner.

"We're clear," said Shimon. "No one is in the building."

Shimon went back into his bag of tricks and took out his lock picks. He went to work on the lock and had the door knob and dead bolt open in thirty seconds. He must have been practicing since the last time I saw him pick a lock because he was even quicker this time. Shimon then reached into his bag and pulled out his hand held device for deactivating alarms. We counted to three and Shimon walked through the door. Within fifteen seconds the alarm was deactivated. Shimon tapped on the door for us to come in. He pulled his laptop from his bag, picked up the signal from the wireless router connected to the computer system and went to work disabling the cameras. It took him three minutes to disable the cameras. The cameras were now on a continuous loop which showed the last image recorded. There would not be any record of our entering the building.

Eytan opened the door and signaled to the team that it was safe for them to enter the building. The four men got out of their car, looked around the area before moving, and headed to the building. They swept the area with their eyes as they walked. Even late at night when there was no one around they took no chances.

When we were all inside, we walked down the corridor into the main area of the building. We were back in the warehouse where Eytan and I saw Officer Mancini meeting with Tony. It was time to get to work.

We assumed that I would be lead down the corridor into the main part of the warehouse to meet with Tony the following evening. There was a second floor which looked out over the first floor where my meeting would likely take place. We looked for the entrance to the second floor and went up there to check if we could use the second floor in our plan. The entrance was visible from the first floor. We would need some cover so the team would not be seen on the second floor. We saw some crates which we moved towards the entrance. We decided the crates would provide adequate cover. We then checked positioning for the rest of the team.

By 1 AM we had worked out the details of our plan. Tony was in for quite a surprise.

Chapter 40

The next morning we got up early and had breakfast at a Jewish deli near our hotel. We did not speak about Tony, the meeting, Murray, or anything related to why we were in New York since one never knew who might be at the next table listening.

After breakfast I called Sergeant O'Leary. He told me to meet him at the police station at 11:30 AM. We went back to the hotel for a bit to pack our luggage and to check out. After checking out, we loaded the cars and headed to the police station. We arrived at 11:25 AM, walked in and asked for Sergeant O'Leary. We were shown into a conference room. We all took seats and waited. A minute later, Sergeant O'Leary walked in with another man.

"Rabbi," said Sergeant O'Leary, "good to see you, although I wish under better circumstances."

"As do I. We appreciate your stepping in to help us," I said.

"I spoke to Agent Thompson from the FBI this morning. From what he tells me about the men sitting around this table, I don't think you need our help. Tony, on the other hand, might need some help."

"We can take care of Tony and we will get Murray back. I want you and Agent Thompson there to take Tony down for what he did. You have been waiting for your chance to get him and I intend to give you that chance."

"Good. Let me introduce Officer Robbins. He and I will lead the NYPD team. We will be ready to take Tony and his gang in if you can deliver something we can make stick in order to prosecute them. We are coordinating our plan with Agent Thompson and the FBI."

We spent thirty minutes going over the plan our team had worked out the night before in Tony's warehouse. The NYPD team would need to stay away from the warehouse until they got the signal that it was clear to approach. We worked out details of how they would be told it was clear so they did not tip off Tony and his gang.

We finished our meeting and Sergeant O'Leary wished us good luck. We shook hands and left the police station.

We went to get lunch and again avoided any discussion of our meeting that evening. At 3 PM we were at the FBI's Manhattan office. We walked into the building and told the woman at the desk that we were there to meet with Agent Thompson. She made a phone call and told us to proceed through the security check. Getting through security took a few minutes. We then took the elevator up to the FBI's office. We got off the elevator, walked into the office and were told to take a seat. Agent Thompson appeared a few moments later.

"Rabbi. Eytan. How are you? I see you brought the whole band with you today."

As stoic and straight faced as Eytan's associates were, that comment elicited a smirk from them.

"Yes I did. We call ourselves the Gefilte Fish Boys. We have quite a dance routine."

"Let's get to work," said Agent Thompson.

We followed Agent Thompson to a conference room. We sat down. Agent Thompson picked up the phone and dialed a number.

"Cynthia, please send Tom in."

A moment later a man appeared who introduced himself as Tom.

"Tom is our electronics expert. He is going to put the wire on you," said Agent Thompson.

I took off my shirt and Tom taped a small microphone to the middle of my chest.

"This is a much smaller microphone than we used back in the old days," I said.

"The technology has dramatically improved," said Tom. "The microphones no longer require a cable and are not as noticeable. These mics are wireless and pick up sound at farther distances and with better clarity. This mic will not be noticeable under your shirt."

"Rabbi, we are also going to give you a bullet proof vest. Based on your plan, we think it best you be covered just in case," said Agent Thompson.

"I suspect my wife would thank you for that."

"This vest is also newer technology. It is lighter, less bulky and stronger. This type of vest is particularly suited to gun shots at close distances. Try it on."

I put on the vest and secured the straps. It was lighter than vests we used when I was a cop. I then put my shirt back on over the vest and mic. The vest was hardly noticeable unless someone knew I was wearing one and was looking for it.

"We have receivers for the mic for everyone in your team, our team and NYPD. We will hear every word you say. When we get the signal, we will go in," said Agent Thompson.

We reviewed the plan with Agent Thompson. Everything seemed to be ready to go. We finished our meeting, left the building and went back to our cars. We headed back to Shimon's office. We decided to leave the weapons and other supplies there until we headed to the meeting with Tony. The less time we were driving around New York with a trunk full of weapons and other military gear, even though if stopped we would eventually get cleared by NYPD and the FBI, the better since any delay would put Murray at risk. I did not get the impression Tony was a patient man, and if I was late for the meeting I did not know what he might do to Murray.

We pulled up to Shimon's office at 6 PM and knocked on the door. He asked for the secret password in Hebrew so I told him "knish". He asked us to hold while he checked the secret password chart. A moment later he opened the door.

"Lucky for you that you gave me the secret password. Otherwise, the rocket launchers on the top floor go off and make for an unpleasant visit," said Shimon.

I laughed but was not entirely sure he was kidding. From the little time I spent with Shimon, it would not surprise me that his office was rigged in some manner to provide for maximum security, which may include rocket launchers.

While Eytan and the rest of the team packed their gear, changed their clothes and got ready, I went into another room and called Tony. Tony picked up on the second ring.

"Tony, this is the Rabbi. I am in New York."

"Glad to hear it Rabbi. Murray will be even happier."

"I have one condition for us to meet," I said.

"I don't think you are in a position to be making demands."

"Perhaps not, but my request is a simple one. If I am to come alone I need to know that Murray is alive. I want a picture of Murray holding up today's newspaper. Make sure that I can see the date in the picture. You can send the picture to my phone."

"Sorry Rabbi. I am not a subscriber to the news-paper. Current events are not my thing," said Tony.

"Fine. Write the word 'Rabbi' on a piece of paper with today's date and have Murray hold that up."

"Stay by your phone."

Tony hung up.

Chapter 41

Tony told Sammy to go get Murray and bring him into the room. Sammy walked into the next room where Murray was tied to a chair. His mouth was taped. Sammy untied Murray's legs, picked him up from the chair, and pushed him to the room that Tony was in.

"Murray. So good to see you. I just spoke with your friend the Rabbi. He would like proof that you are still a living deli owner. Since I do not have today's paper to have you hold as proof, I have written the word Rabbi and today's date as the Rabbi requested. If you would be so kind as to sit in that chair over there, we will take your picture and send it to the Rabbi."

Murray did not make any sound through the tape since he knew there was no point. Sammy pushed Murray into the chair. Sammy handed Murray the piece of paper on which Tony had written. Since Murray's hands were still tied, he held the paper with two fingers on each hand.

"Now hold the paper just below your face and smile pretty for the camera. Oh wait, your mouth is taped so I guess you can't smile too good," Tony said.

Sammy and Guido laughed.

Tony took a picture with his phone, looked at the picture to make sure the date on the paper could be seen, attached the picture to a text message, and sent it to the Rabbi.

"Murray, depending on how things go tonight, that may be the last picture you ever take. It really is a shame you could not smile," remarked Tony.

Murray swallowed hard. Even though he assumed the Rabbi had a plan, he had no idea what was going to happen.

"Your friend the Rabbi is a fool for showing up by himself tonight. He can't protect you. The only question is whether I am going to kill you after I kill him."

Despite being scared, Murray knew that the Rabbi and Eytan were not going to let that happen. If Tony thought the Rabbi was showing up by himself with no backup, Tony was in for a very rude awakening this evening. Despite the tape on his mouth, Murray smiled to himself.

Chapter 42

At 7 PM we loaded the gear into the cars and headed to meet the FBI and NYPD teams. We agreed to meet in an alley ten blocks away from the warehouse. As we pulled into the alley, two vans were there; one from Rocco's Plumbing Service and another from Pete's Locksmith. The signs on the two vans were the cover names we were given by the FBI and NYPD. As our cars pulled in, I put a flashlight out of the driver's side window and flashed the light three times. A moment later a garbage truck pulled in front of the entrance to the alley. Agent Thompson and Sergeant O'Leary stepped out of the two vans. Myself, Eytan and the rest of our team got out of our two cars.

"So it is true. Secret meetings in dark alleys really are as cool as they look in the movies," I said.

"A bit of cover in case anyone is walking by the alley. The driver is one of ours," said Agent Thompson.

Tom got out of the FBI van and approached us.

"Rabbi, we need to check your mic to make sure we are getting good reception," said Tom. Tom handed out ear pieces to everyone who would be entering Tony's warehouse. Everyone put the ear pieces in and waited.

"O.k. Rabbi. I am turning on the mic. Walk to the end of the alley and talk so we can test the mic."

I walked to the end of the alley, turned around and checked with Tom. He gave me the thumbs up that the mic was on.

"Testing, testing. This is Rabbi Klein coming to you live from a dark alley in Manhattan where everyday we play the hits of the 80's, 90's and today here on WRAB, The Rabbi, 104.1 FM."

Tom gave me the thumbs up again that the mic was working. I then walked back to the group.

"Considering what you are about to walk into Rabbi, you have quite the sense of humor," said Agent Thompson.

"Agent, I have nothing to worry about for two reasons. One, I know that Eytan and his team will protect me. Two, if something happens to me, Eytan knows there is no one who can protect him from my wife who will kill him."

"Time to roll," said Agent Thompson. "Everyone get in position. Good luck Rabbi."

Chapter 43

I got into the car by myself. The garbage truck backed away from the entrance to the alley. Eytan and his team got into the other car and drove off. The FBI and NYPD vans drove off as well. I looked at my watch. It was 7:45 PM. I had a few minutes to wait since I figured it would take five minutes to get to Tony's warehouse.

While I waited I said a few prayers. Although I had Eytan and his team, the FBI and NYPD as my backup, I figured some additional backup in the form of divine intervention could only help. I looked at a picture of me with Rachel and the kids which I kept in my wallet. I told myself I would see them soon. I put my gun in my holster. It was time to go.

I pulled out of the alley and headed to the warehouse. I made good time and arrived at 7:57 PM. A man was standing at the door of the warehouse. I got out of the car and walked to the warehouse. I walked up to the man and stood a few feet from him.

"I'm here to see Tony," I said.

"And who are you?"

"I'm The Rabbi."

"Stand there."

The man took out his cell phone and took a picture of me. I did not get the chance to smile, which I figured would not be an issue. The man pushed a few buttons on his phone and told me to wait. I guessed he had sent my picture to Tony to confirm my identity. After thirty seconds the man looked at his phone again.

"You packing?" asked the man.

"Of course."

"Give me the gun."

"You expect me to go in there without my gun. I don't think so," I said.

"Either you give me the gun or you don't go in and your friend likely won't be coming out alive."

I was prepared for this. I purposely put up a fight about my gun to avoid a detailed pat down. If I fought about turning over my gun, it was less likely I would be searched in detail. I slowly opened up the right side of my jacket and took the gun out of my holster. I handed my gun to the man guarding the door.

"Now lift the other side of your jacket," said the man.

I did as I was told.

"Now turn around and lift the back of your jacket."

I did that as well.

"Do I now put my right leg in, my right leg out, my right leg in and shake it all about? I do love the hokey pokey," I said.

"Very funny," said the man. "Now lift your pants legs, one at a time."

I did that as well. His tactic was smart. He was alone. If he patted me down and I tried to make a move to take him out, he would not be in a position to fight if he was searching my pants leg for other guns I might be carrying. Tony was playing it safe.

"Now empty your pockets."

I took out my keys and my cell phone. After the man was satisfied that I was not carrying any other guns, the search was over.

"You can go inside."

"My lucky day," I said.

The man opened the door and I walked into the warehouse. He lead me down the hallway, then we walked into the main part of the warehouse where I had been the night before with Eytan and his team. I looked around acting like it was the first time I had seen the place, when in reality I was checking to make sure that nothing from our set up the night before had been changed. Tony, Sammy and Guido were standing in the middle of the first floor. We stopped a few feet away from where Tony was standing.

"Good evening Rabbi. So nice of you to join us," said Tony.

Chapter 44

Agent Thompson was sitting in the van listening to the exchange between the Rabbi and the man at the door of the warehouse. A moment later he heard a voice over his walkie talkie. As a precaution, he had agents posted on rooftops for the few blocks leading up to the warehouse to make sure the path would be clear for the FBI, NYPD, and Eytan's team to drive the few blocks to the warehouse.

"Sir, we have a problem. About two blocks away from the warehouse we have a car that just pulled up. Two men got out and are sitting on either side of the car. From the looks of them they are with the Balduccis."

"Damn," said Agent Thompson. "Tony is watching the road to make sure the Rabbi went in alone. We need to get those guys out of there quietly."

Agent Thompson grabbed a second walkie talkie and pressed the talk button.

"Eytan, we have a problem. Two guys pulled up two

blocks from the warehouse. Our eyes on the roof just spotted them. They appear to be some of Tony's guys who are probably watching to make sure the Rabbi went in alone and that no one is coming in behind him. We need them out of there."

"We will take care of it," said Eytan.

Eytan addressed all of the men in the car with him.

"O.k., you heard Agent Thompson. Avi, you come with me. Here is the plan," said Eytan.

Once they worked out the details, Eytan and Avi got out of the car. They left their guns in the car since guns would draw attention. They got out of the car and walked the two blocks to where the car was with Tony's two lookouts. As they turned the corner, Eytan and Avi saw the car. The two men were leaning against the car on the passenger side. While they looked bored, it was clear they were watching the street for signs of trouble. Eytan and Avi walked up to the two men.

"Excuse me. My cousin and I are visiting from Egypt. We are looking for a Middle Eastern restaurant that is supposed to be around here called Abdullah's Magic Carpet. Do you know of it?" asked Eytan.

"Hey Vinnie, you ever hear of that place?"

"No, I am not a fan of Mediterranean food."

"Sorry fellas, we can't help you. We are sort of in the middle of something here, so if you could move along we would appreciate it."

"No problem," said Eytan. "Thanks for your help."

Eytan and Avi then hit the two men and knocked them both out. The two men slumped against the side of the car. Eytan opened the driver side door and popped the trunk. He and Avi lifted the two men into the trunk and closed it.

"They will be safe here for now. Let's get back to the car," said Eytan.

Eytan and Avi ran back to the car. Eytan picked up his walkie talkie.

"We're good. The look outs are taking a nap in the trunk of the car. When this is done you can go back and pick them up."

"Thanks," said Agent Thompson. "Time for Phase 1. Eytan, you're up again. We lost time with the men in the car. Get moving."

Eytan drove the car within one block of the warehouse. The vans followed behind him. Eytan parked the car and he and Avi got out. They put their guns on their hip holsters and ran to the corner. Eytan took the walkie talkie from his belt.

"Is the door clear?" he asked.

"One second," said Agent Thompson.

After Agent Thompson got the all clear signal from the lookouts on the roof, he told Eytan it was clear. Eytan and Avi ran to the door of the warehouse and waited. Less than a minute later the man who searched the Rabbi opened the door. When he closed the door, Eytan and Avi were pointing their guns at his face.

"Who are you two?" asked the man.

"One more word and it will be your last," said Eytan.

Eytan hit the man in the stomach and then hit him in the back of the neck. The man dropped on the ground unconscious. Two men jumped out of the FBI van, ran up to the door of the warehouse, put zip tie plastic handcuffs on the man and dragged him to the van. The FBI and NYPD teams got out of the vans. The remaining three men in Eytan's team got out of the car. The two FBI agents loaded the unconscious door man into the van, put zip tie cuffs on his legs, a piece of tape across his mouth and closed the door. Everyone who was going into the warehouse checked their equipment and took their guns off of safety. They ran to the door of the warehouse to join Eytan and Avi.

Eytan and his team would be the first to enter the warehouse so that they could get in position. Shimon would go in with Eytan's team. The FBI and NYPD teams would wait in the hallway for the signal that either everything was clear or that there was trouble. On the count of three Eytan's team quietly entered the warehouse.

Chapter 45

"It is unfortunate that you have chosen to act this way Tony. You may remember when we first met that I told you the most important thing is respect. Taking Murray the way you did is a sign of great disrespect to me and my business associates. They do not take kindly to such things," I said.

"Rabbi, this is business. By refusing my very generous offer of fifteen percent you insulted me. Insulting me is not very good for your business. The Balduccis get what they want Rabbi, one way or the other."

"Well, before we get to that Tony, I want to see Murray. Bring him out here."

Tony turned his head towards the hallway.

"Yo, Gino. Bring Murray over here."

A few seconds later Murray walked into the main part of the warehouse followed by a man in an expensive Italian suit who I presumed was Gino.

"Here he is boss. You want me to stay here?" asked Gino.

"Sure Gino. Stick around."

Murray's hands were tied, but he looked o.k. Murray did not have a black eye or any bruises that were noticeable which meant that Tony hopefully had not beaten up on him. Murray's eyes lit up when he saw me. He knew if I was here, Eytan and his team were close by as well.

"See Rabbi, Murray is fine. We did not rough him up or anything."

"How did you get him to New York Tony? Did you drive him up here yourself?"

"Drive? What are you crazy? Murray took a nap and found his way into a container that found its way onto a cargo plane that went from Miami to New York."

"So you drugged Murray and put him on a cargo plane to take him up here. Did he at least get a meal on the plane or a free movie to watch?"

"Funny guy you are Rabbi."

"I hear that a lot."

"Murray was quite comfortable on the cargo plane I put him on to get to New York. Anyway, here is the deal Rabbi. If you and Murray want to walk out of here in one piece, you are going to give me what I want and you are lucky that I am still offering you fifteen percent. I should make it ten percent since you have caused me so much trouble."

"Before I comment on your very generous offer Tony, tell me, why do you really want to buy knishes from Murray? It isn't because you want to get into selling ethnic foods, now is it?"

"My reasons are of no concern to you."

"I think your reasons are very much my concern. You are not really interested in making money off of Murray's knishes. You intend to use them in your drug business. And since that business is far more profitable than the food business, your offer of a portion of the food sale profits is not a genuine offer. It is not nice to try to pull the wool over the eyes of the Israeli mob Tony. Bad things can happen if you do that."

"I don't know what you are talking about."

"Really Tony? You are not a very good liar. I figured out what you are up to Tony. You are using the ethnic foods you are purchasing to throw off the drug sniffing dogs. You figured out that certain ethnic foods throw off their ability to sniff out the drugs which you are shipping around the country."

"Very good Rabbi. You are not as dumb as you look. It's brilliant. We get to ship our drugs without worrying that the dogs will pick up what is really in the containers."

While Tony was talking, three members of Eytan's team made their way up to the second floor of the warehouse and got into position. Eytan and Avi made their way behind where Tony and his crew were standing on the first floor.

"Since you figured out my plan Rabbi we now have a problem. I don't think you will be getting out of here alive. I can't have you running around with knowledge of what I am doing. My plan is worth an enormous amount of money and I cannot have you interfering. With you gone, Murray won't have any other business partners to answer to and he will get me all the knishes I need," said Tony.

"Tony, you think you are going to knock off a member of the Israeli mafia and walk away clean? Perhaps you are dumber than you look."

"I don't respond well to calling me names."

"And I don't respond well to threats to kill me. Seems we each have things that bother us Tony."

"Well, I think you will respond quite badly to being

shot numerous times," said Tony.

Sammy, Guido and Gino pulled out their guns and pointed them at me.

Eytan heard Tony's threat and knew it was time for his team to make their move. Shimon who was also listening in knew it too. Shimon dialed the Rabbi's pay as you go cell phone. The Rabbi felt the phone vibrate in his pocket. He knew Eytan was going to make his move momentarily.

"Tony, I am a religious man. Since you are pointing three guns at me, I think I need to pray."

"Since you will be meeting your maker soon, I think I can grant your last wish," said Tony.

I got on my knees, put my hands together and started mumbling a prayer.

A few seconds later the lights went out.

"Hey, what's going on?" asked Tony.

They fired their guns.

Chapter 46

When the lights went out, I fell onto my back and rolled to the right. Eytan's team on the second floor had night vision goggles on. When they saw I was safely out of the way, they fired their guns. Each of their guns had silencers so the shots were not heard over Tony asking what was happening. Eytan's team members were expert marksmen. They each fired at the guns held by Sammy, Guido and Gino and shot the guns right out of their hands.

Now it was Eytan's turn. He and Avi, who were also wearing night vision goggles, moved in from behind Tony and his crew. They first punched Sammy and Guido in the face. Then Eytan and Avi moved to the side. Not knowing that Eytan and Avi were out of the way, Sammy and Guido each threw punches and hit each other in the face and stumbled back. Eytan then kicked Gino in the stomach. As Gino leaned over, Eytan and Avi punched Sammy and Guido in their sides with three quick punches. Sammy and Gino fell to the floor. Eytan, who was then behind Tony, tapped Tony on his shoulder. When Tony turned around, Eytan punched Tony in his face and kneed him in his stomach.

Sammy then got off of the floor and threw a punch in Avi's direction. Avi blocked the punch and caught Sammy's wrist. Avi then stepped to Sammy's right side and twisted Sammy's wrist which caused him to scream out in pain. Avi kneed Sammy in his stomach and kicked Sammy's leg out from under him so that he fell hard to the floor. Gino then came racing at Eytan with his arms outstretched hoping he might grab someone who was throwing all of the punches. Before Gino got close, Eytan kicked Sammy in his stomach, kicked him in his knee and then stomped on his right foot. Sammy went down writhing in pain.

Tony, who by this time was recovering from being hit, threw two wild punches not knowing which direction his attackers may be facing. Eytan stepped back to avoid the first punch, stepped into Tony to block the second punch and then smacked Tony open-handed in both of his ears. The shot to his ears threw off Tony's equilibrium so he stumbled back. Avi, who was standing behind Tony tripped Tony who then fell to the floor.

Guido then started throwing punches hoping he might hit someone. Avi blocked one of the punches and grabbed Guido's wrist, stepped to the side, elbowed Guido in the ribs, punched him in his kidney and pulled Guido's arm up so that it bent at the elbow. As Guido began to lose his balance, Avi pulled Guido's elbow back towards the floor and kicked Guido's right leg out from under him. Guido fell to the ground.

After leaving Tony and his crew a crumpled heap on the floor, Eytan and Avi quickly went back to the area from where they came so they could make their way out of the warehouse.

Agent Thompson and his team then moved into the main part of the warehouse along with the NYPD team. The lights came back on.

"FBI and NYPD," said Agent Thompson. "Hands in the air."

Tony and his crew were shaking their heads trying to figure out what had just happened. I was back up on my knees. Murray had not moved from where he had been sitting. He also looked confused about what had just happened.

"Tony," said Agent Thompson, "you and your boys are under arrest."

"For what?" asked Tony. "We are having a meeting. That is not illegal."

"Let's see Tony. How about we start with kidnapping across state lines. And then there is your plan to use ethnic foods to throw off drug sniffing dogs so that you can ship drugs around the country," said Agent Thompson.

"What are you talking about?" said Tony.

"Tony, you kidnapped the knish king of Miami Beach who is sitting over there and you are meeting with the Rabbi, head of the Israeli mob's Miami Beach outfit. You want to play dumb, or be as dumb as you apparently are, that's fine. We know what you have been up to Tony. We have been waiting a long time to take you down, and I can assure you that you are going down for this one. As an added bonus, you have given us the Rabbi and Murray who has been doing business with the Israeli mob."

"We'll see about that. My lawyers will have us out in a few hours," said Tony.

"Cuff them and get them out of here," said Agent Thompson.

The FBI agents moved in and put hand cuffs on Tony, Guido, Sammy and Gino. Then they put hand cuffs on Murray and I. They walked all of us out of the warehouse. More vehicles had arrived since I went into the warehouse. Tony and his gang were loaded into a van. Murray and I were put into the back of a car which Agent Thompson was driving. The back of the van Tony was loaded into was purposely left open so Tony could see Murray and I being driven away by the FBI. When we were around the corner, Murray broke his silence.

"Rabbi, thank you for saving me. I thought they were going to kill me. I don't know how I can ever repay you," said Murray.

"Well, you have a lot of people to thank aside from me. Eytan and some of his friends did the shooting and punching, and the FBI and NYPD were in on the plan as well to take down Tony and his gang."

"I think it came off as believable," said Agent Thompson. "Tony will think that we are taking both of you in and charging you as well. NYPD has someone down at the courthouse getting a search warrant for Tony's warehouse. I am sure we will find plenty of additional evidence in there to support multiple charges."

"What about Officer Mancini?" I asked.

"We spoke with him and he came clean. We are not sure what crime he can be charged with for allowing his dog to be used to test if ethnic foods can throw off drug sniffing dogs. Even if he is charged, he has agreed to testify against the Balduccis, and I suspect that in exchange for his testimony he will get off without any jail time. He will have to leave New York and go into the witness protection program because he will be at risk even if we dismantle the Balduccis's network in the northeast."

I asked Agent Thompson if we could pull over and remove the hand cuffs so I could call Rachel. Once the hand cuffs were off, I called her and told her that Murray and I were safe. She was relieved and said she could not wait for me to get home. Murray then called Deborah and told her he was safe. I could hear her scream with joy even though the phone was a few feet away from me. As much as I liked New York, I decided I had enough of the Big Apple for a while. It was time to go home.

Chapter 47

Agent Thompson took Murray and I to Shimon's office to meet up with Eytan and his team. We needed to return the guns and equipment to Shimon and thought it best to do so while law enforcement officials were not around. When Murray walked into Shimon's office, he thanked every member of the team, told everyone they were welcome at his deli any time, and that the food was on him.

We packed up our things and headed to the airport. While we were waiting for our flight I called Agent Thompson to check in with him.

"We got the search warrant and NYPD is going through the warehouse. They have already found a significant amount of drugs. I expect they will find more useful items and documents in their search. We also checked the tape from the wire you were wearing. The recording quality is perfect. We have Tony's confession to kidnapping and his plan to use ethnic foods to throw off drug sniffing dogs. That will get him a conspiracy charge. Between the federal and state charges, Tony is facing serious jail time. You did good Rabbi. You took down the Balduccis. The FBI owes you one," said Agent Thompson.

"Happy to help and I thank you for helping us get Murray back. If something happened to him his wife would have killed me."

"Murray is lucky to have a friend like you Rabbi. Have a safe flight back to Miami. When things settle down, give me a call and we will get coffee."

"The usual place," I said.

"Where else?" said Agent Thompson. He then hung up.

I looked at Eytan and his associates sitting with Murray. These men, who did not even know Murray, were willing to endanger themselves to get him back. While they were trained for such things, and had probably done so countless times while working for the Mossad, their actions were a testament to who we are as Jews. When there is a need, we help.

A few minutes later we boarded the plane. Murray was exhausted so he went right to sleep. I got a bit of sleep myself. We landed at Miami International

Airport at 3 AM. After Eytan and his associates got their bags, Murray and I thanked them again for their help and they headed to their car. Eytan, Murray and I then headed to my car. I dropped Murray off at his house. I then drove to Eytan's house. I pulled into the driveway and parked.

"Thank you again for having my back in New York. You're a good friend Eytan."

"And I am a former or current Mossad agent which I can neither confirm nor deny."

"Get out of my car. Get out right now," I said while smiling. "I don't care whether you are currently or used to be with the Mossad. You saved Murray and that is all that matters."

"We saved Murray Rabbi. You were the one facing three Italian mobsters with guns. I merely had to render them semi-conscious. Go home and get some rest Rabbi."

I pulled out of Eytan's driveway and drove to my house. I parked the car, grabbed my bag and opened the door. Rachel was waiting for me on our new couch. She ran to the door and hugged me for a while before speaking.

"Moshe. I'm so glad you're safe. I was so worried."

"Worrying is your thing Rachel. You're good at it."

"You must invite Eytan and his associates over for dinner so I can thank them personally."

"Eytan never argues with the chance to eat a meal cooked by you, so that should be easy."

We sat down on the couch and I told Rachel about everything that had happened, how we set up our plan to take down Tony and his gang, what happened inside the warehouse and how Murray and I were put under pretend arrest to convince Tony and his crew that the Israeli mob story was legitimate so that Murray would be left alone.

"So three of them pulled their guns on you?" asked Rachel.

"Yes they did, but I had three expert marksman from the Mossad protecting me and I was wearing a bullet proof vest."

Rachel sat and thought for a moment.

"You put yourself at great risk to save Murray. That was very brave of you."

"All in a day's work for Super Rabbi," I said.

"Well Super Rabbi, your family is very happy to have you home safe."

Rachel and I sat on the couch for a few minutes.

"I am going upstairs. When you are ready, come to bed. You must be exhausted."

Rachel looked at me and kissed me. She then got off of the couch and started walking up the stairs. Half way up the stairs she stopped.

"By the way, we are getting a new T.V. It will go well with the new couch."

Rachel then continued walking up the stairs.

I sat on the couch for a minute. I knew how Murray could repay me. He was buying me a new T.V.

The End

Sort of. Some books end with the author providing the first few pages of their new book as a teaser of what is to come next. I have chosen to go in the opposite direction. I am going to take you back in time to 1994. The reason we are going back to 1994 is because it was in that year that I wrote my first Jewish themed story. I was taking an American Humor class as part of my attempt to obtain an English degree after I graduated from college so that I could teach high school English for a few years. For one class assignment we had to write a tall tale. I was not sure what to write, and then one day it hit me—a story about a man who is looking for a hobby and through divine intervention is sent on a quest to challenge a Rabbi, who is the greatest shuffleboard player in the world, to a match. But what would I call it? Then, it hit me again—Shuffleboard, Bagels and Lox: Oy!

My story was well received in class. The following

year I had given up on my pursuit of an English degree and was then obtaining a paralegal degree. I saw an announcement that the school's chapter of Sigma Tau Delta—the International English Honor Society—was having a writing competition. I decided to submit my story. I won the award for one of the categories, which if I recall was the best comedy story.

Now, the circle is complete. I started with a Rabbi who was the world's greatest shuffleboard player, and now I have written a book about a Rabbi who is a private investigator.

So, without further adieu, I give you my award winning story—Shuffleboard, Bagels and Lox: Oy!

Shuffleboard, Bagels and Lox: Oy!
(A Tall Tale)

The ship was a glorious one, bigger than any other they had ever been on. As the old men sat on the deck drinking their scotches, the oldest of the bunch said:

"Boys, I want to tell you about a great man, a champion among men."

"Who is this person? Is he a Rabbi?" inquired Moshe.

"Is he a Jew? He must be a Jew" said Yossi.

"Zzzzzz . . . Zzzzzz . . . Hey what you wake me for? I'm sleeping over here," yelled Morris.

"This man was named Menachem Rabinowitz Ben Noah Rubinstein Shalom Alechem Schwartz. The greatest shuffleboard player to ever live," declared Shlomi.

As Shlomi said the great man's name, the heavens roared triumphantly. Morris, now awake, said:

"With this many names he must be a great man, but was he circumcised?"

Shlomi began his story.

A long time ago, Menachem Schwartz lived on a hill

in the mountains. Menachem was bored and decided he needed a hobby. Being a man of deep religious faith, Menachem decided that he would consult the bible. Menachem looked in Leviticus XV, chapter 12. After reading about how to run a kosher deli, Menachem tried Judges, Lawyers and Insurance, chapter 16. In that chapter there was the story of a man who was bored with life. The man searched for years to find something to amuse himself. He finally found the answer through the Lord. One night, the Lord visited this man and told him he should take up . . . The next page was ripped out of his bible. Menachem cursed the traveling goy salesman who sold it to him and swore to only buy bibles from Jews from now on.

Menachem then decided to try a different approach. For the next ten days, Menachem ate nothing but Twinkies and drank Colt 45 beer until he was deathly ill. Lying on his bed near death, he had a vision one night while sleeping.

Crash, Boom, crack.

"Hey, who's there?" asked Menachem.

"It is I, Moses. The man who brought the Jews through the desert and brought them to the holy land of Israel."

"But it took you forty years to get there," said Menachem.

"Hey, the desert is a big place. We got lost. We left the map behind in Egypt and got bad directions from some gypsies. Have you ever tried carrying two stone tablets of commandments? I bet you would have a bad back too. Oy. Everybody's a critic."

"Well, Moses, what are you doing here?" asked Menachem.

"I have come to give you the answer that you seek," Moses declared.

"Yes. Please tell me," pleaded Menachem.

"Buy stock in Disney. They have got a bright future."

"You imbecile. I am looking for a hobby, not stock tips!" yelled Menachem.

"Oh sorry. Wrong message. The Almighty Himself has told me that you are to become the world's greatest shuffleboard player."

"Shuffleboard! I ate Twinkies and drank bad beer for this? I should have just called the psychic hotline. I am not eighty years old and living in a retirement community in Miami. I am not playing shuffleboard."

"Menachem, it is not wise to disobey the Lord. Do you remember Jimmy Hoffa? He got the same message as you and refused. The Lord turned him into an obnoxious, loudmouth talk show host who criticizes politicians and deserves to be hung with his own shoelaces."

"You mean Rush Limbaugh?" asked Menachem.

"Yes. You know the man. Horrible existence. Anyway, heed the word of the Lord, use the force and fulfill your destiny Luke. Oh wait. That's the wrong story," said Moses.

Suddenly, Moses vanished into thin air. Menachem decided that if he was going to be shuffleboard champion he needed somewhere to practice. Menachem began clearing the ground with his huge hands until he had a 10 by 20 foot area. He then ripped 50 foot trees out of the ground with his bare hands and threw them up in the air. As the trees came down, he would hit the trees with his mighty arms and slice the trees into perfectly even 2x4's.

Once he collected the wood, Menachem laid each piece down on the ground, side by side. Menachem squeezed sections of the wood so tightly that the wood stuck together without any nails. Menachem then grabbed the nearest bear, ripped the fur right off of its body, and sanded down the shuffleboard track until it had a bright shine.

Menachem next began a rigid practice schedule for forty days and forty nights. Through sleet, snow, sun and rain, he would be out there practicing. During a horrible rainstorm one evening, Noah and his ark passed by. Noah asked Menachem if he wanted to join him and the boys on a trip to a local bar in town to try to convince some women that the world was coming to an end and that G-d told them to take a ride on Noah's ark. Menachem, although tempted, declined for he knew that he was on a mission.

After the fortieth night, Menachem was sitting on his bed resting from his practice. He then heard a noise.

"Hey, who's there? Moses, if that is you again you need to work on your entrances. They are way too noisy."

Out of the corner appeared a short man in a toga and glasses.

"Hey, you're Woody Allen. I have seen all of your movies."

"No kid. I'm the G-d of Shuffleboard in this story. Work has been tough ever since the split with Mia, so my agent got me this part. Have you ever wondered how women can go to the mall for eight hours and shop and not buy anything?"

"Well Woody, I mean G-d of Shuffleboard, what are you doing here?"

"I have come to give you the tool you will need to become the greatest shuffleboard champion to ever live," said Woody.

In Woody's outstretched arms appeared a golden shuffleboard stick.

"Take this stick and go down to the city. There you will find the man you must beat and you will defeat the empire and Darth Vader. Oops, wrong story. Also, your mother has been asking why you never call her anymore. Good luck young jedi."

Menachem packed up his things and headed into town. He could feel the hand of Fate around his neck, and he was beginning to choke, so he asked Mr. Fate to not squeeze so tightly.

Menachem had heard about the greatest shuffleboard player in town, Rabbi Shlemecki. Although Rabbi Shlemecki was 80 years old, he could destroy any man, woman, or child at shuffleboard, and he made a mean bagel and lox. When Menachem reached the town, he asked some of the people where Rabbi Shlemecki could be found.

"Oh, you have heard of the Rabbi's bagel and lox!" they said.

"No," replied Menachem, "I have come to challenge him at shuffleboard."

The townspeople laughed so hard that they nearly lost their matzah balls. Menachem found the Rabbi's temple and entered his chambers.

"Rabbi Shlemecki. I hear you are the shuffleboard champion, but I have come to challenge you!"

"Are you one of those Christians or Hari-Krishna people?"

"No I am the greatest shuffleboard player in all the land!" declared Menachem.

"Boychick, did you get knocked on the skull? Do you have a fever? Read that sign."

The sign read: "Rabbi Shlemecki, the greatest shuffleboard player to ever live, and maker of a damn good bagel and lox." Menachem was not impressed.

"If you are truly a champion, you will accept my challenge."

"Oy, gefilte fish! I tell you. Kids today. All right. I accept your challenge. But first, would you like a bagel and lox?"

Off they went to the center of town where Rabbi

Shlemecki had built his own shuffleboard track. As they walked through the town, a crowd began to follow them. When they got to the shuffleboard track, Menachem took out his golden stick. The Rabbi then took out his stick. Up and down the Rabbi's stick were different titles he had won and names of people he had beaten. This was a very impressive stick.

"Sonny boy," said Rabbi Shlemecki, "you may go first."

Menachem stretched a little, walked up to the board, and with the force of ten Arkansas bears flung the puck.

"Not bad," said Rabbi Shlemecki. "You must have a good Jewish grandmother who fed you lots of chicken noodle soup."

The game was a fierce one. The two men were tied neck and neck in scoring most of the match. The crowd was buzzing with excitement. It was the last shot of the game and Menachem was down by three points.

"This it, bubbalah," said the Rabbi. "Your last chance to beat the champion, that is if you do not choke. I will now put a curse on you and your next ten generations."

Suddenly, Woody Allen appeared.

"Menachem, you can do it. Use the force. You are my son."

Menachem focused all of his energy on this shot, but he was concerned about the revelation regarding his father. Was he to going to become infatuated with eighteen year old Chinese girls? On the next Jerry Springer, children of movie stars who play shuffleboard and like young Oriental women. As he flung the puck, the crowd was knocked off their feet by the force of his concentration. He scored five points and became champion.

"Well, you beat me," said Rabbi Shlemecki. "One would think you would respect your elders and lose, but no. As I said, kids today! What can you do? I am proud of you and it is actually nice to be beaten. I have been champion for forty years. Anyway, would you like a bagel and lox?"